Plateful of Murder

A Terrified Detective Mystery

Carole Fowkes

Cover Design: Kathleen Baldwin
Copy Edited by Michelle Morrow
formatting by Ink Lion Books
Release date: January 2016

Chapter One

Michael Adler had no idea when he first walked into my cramped, West Side of Cleveland office that the only investigating I'd done involved getting the goods on cheating spouses. Working a criminal case went beyond my career goals. Besides, my Master's degree in Mass Communications didn't include any courses on fighting the underworld.

Still, I was thrilled with the potential of a new client, a rarity for my agency. Those who did employ me were for the most part paunchy, middle-aged men with unfaithful trophy wives. Something told me this guy, who was as tall and thin as a strand of spaghetti, wasn't looking to find out some dirt on a cheating lover.

"Can I help you?"

My potential client's eyes darted around the room. "I'm Michael Adler. Is this Gino Francini Investigations?"

I jumped up from my office chair, banging my knee against my desk. "Yes, and I'm Claire DeNardo, chief private investigator." I stood as tall as my 5'2" frame allowed. "What can I do for you?"

I gestured to the worn chair by my desk and studied him. Pale face, mid-thirties, losing his hair but trying to disguise it. Black-rimmed glasses, fish-bowl thick. No wedding ring.

He pushed back an errant strand of hair. "My sister, Constance, is a manager at Triton Pharmaceuticals at W.115th and Detroit. She's very accomplished, but she doesn't exactly..." He cleared his throat. "Have good people skills."

"Can you, um, be more specific?"

"She may have rubbed someone the wrong way." He pulled a couple of wrinkled letters from his jacket. "These are the second and third threats she's received."

I read the top note aloud. "You'll be sorry if you do the wrong thing." The other had a similar theme. Both were blunt enough to give me an unpleasant worminess in my stomach. "Have you taken these to the police?"

He nodded. "The first letter. They said we should take it up with Triton's human resources department."

A headache crept from the back of my head to my temples. "Was the first letter along these same lines?"

"Yes. Except it told her to do the right thing before it was too late." His Adam's apple shifted on his long, Ichabod Crane neck. He pushed his glasses up with his index finger.

My potential client closed his eyes, took a deep breath, and folded his hands in his lap. His eyelids fluttered, and he picked up where he left off. "I'd have brought you the first letter as well, but I don't know what she did with it."

Something was missing. Why was he here instead of Constance? "Why didn't your sister come to me with this? Or at least come *with* you?"

His face flushed, making the scarcity of his white-blond hair even more noticeable. "She refuses to pay some stranger to do what she thinks she can do herself."

I gritted my teeth. The average Jane watches a few detective shows on television and figures she can battle crime too. Someone should write an exposé on every wannabe detective who catches the criminal without so much as messing up her tight, see-my-cleavage outfit. "Does your sister have a plan?"

"Something unwise, I'm sure." He took off his glasses and rubbed his eyes.

Not bad-looking without his super-thick spectacles.

He clenched his jaw. "She doesn't seem to realize the danger she's in. I love my sister, but sometimes she's so stubborn. She thinks she can bulldoze her way through anything." He paused. "Please. Money is no object. I recently sold my business at a huge profit." He turned even pinker. "My apologies. I didn't mean to brag." His expression was similar to a puppy caught chewing his owner's shoe. With the Gino Francini Agency showing no sign of growth and a lot of bills going unpaid, Mr. Adler suddenly had my rapt attention.

I've always held a strong belief life should be fair. More than the-same-size-pie-slice fair. I wanted justice, the kind everyone no matter how rich or poor deserved. Maybe the countless old gangster movies I watched with my mother created then fed my desire. Every time a bad guy got filled with lead I cheered. While other girls played with dolls, I played get-the-crook. Of course, the hero was always me, hauling the scumbag to jail and recovering the stolen purse containing the elderly victim's entire life's savings.

Right now, that itch to help the helpless and keep

things balanced needed scratching. Plus, if I didn't get an inflow of cash soon, I'd be living out of my 1998 Toyota, Bob. Bob was a good car and although he was pretty comfortable, I didn't relish making him my home on wheels.

But this case was scary enough to make me want to hide under my desk. Not that being afraid was something new. Lots of things terrified me from childhood. Balloons bursting, roller coasters, hairpieces, even getting big hips like my aunt's.

My gut screamed for me to recommend another PI. Dealing with an ocean of tears and denials from cheating spouses was one thing. Stepping between a crazed letter writer and his intended victim made my mind see the word, *danger*, in flashing lights.

Ultimately, my desire for justice and desperate need for money held sway over my decision. To clamp down on any rising sense of foreboding, I told myself whoever sent these letters probably wouldn't be armed with anything more than a stapler. "Okay. I'll take your case."

He gave me a relieved smile, pulled his sister's photo from his wallet and laid it on my desk. She was pretty, in a snooty sort of way. She looked like the kind of woman who cuts someone out of her life if they belch out loud. Blonde hair pulled back tight. High cheekbones. Except for the similar coloring, I wouldn't have guessed she and Michael Adler were brother and sister.

He filled me in on the details of her daily routine.

When he concluded I asked, "How do you want me to proceed?" My hope was he'd want me to shadow his sister and report back to him on anybody acting suspicious. Surveillance work suited me. Most of the people I shadowed weren't even aware of being observed until the incriminating photos showed up. Being invisible was my biggest talent.

Adler's light, almost white, eyebrows knitted. "We should set up a meeting with you and Constance. If she found out I had you protecting her without her knowledge, she would crucify me."

I took a deep breath to calm myself. The author of the letters could just as easily be some nerdy mail clerk who got mad when Constance refused to lick her own envelopes.

"Okay, Mr. Adler. Let's meet at The Irishman's Café on West 140th and Detroit Avenue at 6:00 tonight."

"Please call me Michael. Constance and I will both be there." He wouldn't get a ribbon for enthusiasm. Still, he put half down. The rest of the payment would come when I found the Ernest Hemingway who wrote those letters to Constance.

The remainder of my day was spent shuffling papers and mulling over my budget. I deposited Adler's check and arrived at the café a bit before 6:00.

By 6:30, no Michael and Constance Adler, and, what remained of my tea, had grown cold. I was on my way out when Michael called. He sounded hysterical.

"Constance. She's dead." His breath caught. "I went to her office to pick her up. It was torn apart and…" He sobbed. "Please, come."

My mouth fell open. Those letters hadn't been idle threats. "Michael, where are you?" I kept my voice firm to push through his sorrow and shock. "Did you call the police?"

"In Triton's lobby. Police are in her office. I need your help."

Every molecule of my skittish innards told me to

refund his money and go back to finding cheaters. But Michael's grief-stricken plea touched my heart. "I'll be there in fifteen minutes." Unable to stop myself I added, "That is, if you're sure you really, really want me to come."

He did.

Chapter Two

On the way over, I rehearsed how to back out of our contract. I was scared. Now that this case had morphed into a murder investigation, I wanted out. The police could handle Constance's slaying. My role would be to offer my sincere condolences and a full refund.

Fearfulness was a familiar feeling. I come from a long line of anxious Italian women. My mother's screams of "Don't do that, you'll hurt yourself," still ring in my ears.

It might seem strange for someone as faint of heart as I am to be a PI, but my investigatory career started with me playing the part of an administrative assistant to my father's second cousin, Gino Francini, who owned the PI firm. Later, Gino taught me how to take pictures of people in situations they shouldn't have been in. Patience and a good long-range lens were the only things needed. That suited me fine.

Two years ago, Gino got tired of the harsh Cleveland winters and retired to Miami. He left the agency to me. Since my Master's degree in Mass Communications didn't put me high up on any employer's list, I took it on.

Not that it was much at that point. The profitable worker's compensation cases had slipped through Gino's fingers after he got into a fistfight with a deadbeat, claiming a back injury. Since I'd been the one photographing cheating spouses, it made sense for me to carry on the business. Despite some dry spells, it was enough for me to eke out a living without jeopardizing my life.

But staying on this case put me too near that line between making a living and getting killed. The most danger I cared to face was driving through the wild and busy intersection at W. 25th and Clark.

Then, one look at Michael convinced me resigning from his sister's case just then would be cruel. Poor guy looked like someone took out his spine and left his body to flop about. Sort of like those balloon men snapping in the wind at grand openings of car dealerships. His red-rimmed eyes and drooping shoulders showed the depth of his sorrow. Sympathy tears sprang to my eyes and I blinked them back. I'm a hugger but this time I restrained myself. "Michael, please accept my condolences."

Poor guy reminded me of Raymond, a kid in my third-grade class everyone picked on. That boy also wore thick glasses. I should have stood up for him. Before he climbed that tree to escape and fell. Fear stopped me, like it had so many times since. Maybe helping Michael Adler would be my chance at redemption.

The guy with Michael, looking every inch a police detective with his strong jaw and 'sweat a confession out of them' attitude, spoke up. "And you are?"

I peered into the bluest eyes I'd ever seen outside of a Paul Newman movie. Too bad their owner was staring at me over a dead body. Any other time I'd be batting my eyelashes for all they were worth. *Better to play it straight.* "Claire DeNardo. Mr. Adler hired me to protect his sister."

I could've sworn he muttered, "Yeah, hell of a job." The scowl on his face was loud and clear. "Don't get in my way." He flashed his badge. "Detective Corrigan, Cleveland PD. This is our investigation now."

Michael blew his nose and focused his eyes on me. "I should've hired you after the first letter." The muscles in his jaw tensed. "Although if the police had taken that letter as a serious threat, there would have been no need to hire you at all." Sorrow mixed with anger rippled through his last words.

The detective kept his voice low, sort of like a psychiatrist with a gone-off-his-meds patient. "The best thing we can do now is find out who did this and lock them up." Corrigan glanced at his notes. "One last question, Mr. Adler. Do you know why your sister's office was tossed or what he or she was looking for?"

Michael stared off into the distance. "No idea."

Detective Corrigan studied him for a minute, put his notepad away and pulled a business card from his pocket. "If you remember anything else call me." With an eyebrow cocked, he nodded to me, turned and strutted off.

Gentle as an undertaker, I asked, "Michael, is there anyone you can stay with tonight?"

He gazed down. "It's only me now. Parents died years ago."

My family flashed through my mind. I couldn't fathom having no one. It would be so…quiet, and not in a good way.

Before I thought it through, I was offering to have a

drink with him. God, someone should've reported me to the bad PI league. Rule number one, according to Gino: "Pity is a real sucker's game." He must have known I'd be tempted to get involved on a personal level with a client.

Once at the bar, I sighed and vowed to make the drink a quick one. Ignoring another of my fears, getting hips like my aunt, I ordered a chocolate martini.

He ordered a single malt bourbon, then stared down at his hands. "I can't believe she's gone."

Despite his quivering chin, he picked up his drink and managed to drain it. "If I'd just gotten to her office sooner." He slammed the glass down on the table so hard my drink sloshed a bit over the rim.

"You would've been killed, too."

He waved my comment away. "The police will never find the killer."

Poor guy. I patted his forearm. "Maybe not tomorrow, but they will."

"I suppose you'll want to drop the case now that she's dead?"

"Michael, I told you when you hired me this might be a matter for the police. Now with Constance murdered, it definitely is."

"You're saying this case is too dangerous and I agree."

I opened my mouth to resign, but my relentless sense of justice wouldn't stay out of it. I found myself saying, "I'd still like to remain involved." That was my heart, the ole softy, speaking. It remembered Michael was alone.

He frowned. "I'd rather you didn't." He added, "Don't misunderstand. You seem like a nice lady. Not a hardboiled private investigator. If something catastrophic happened, having your life on my conscience would be too much."

A nice lady? If I couldn't hold my own as an effective PI, Gino should have given the agency to his gambling, big-talking nephew, Little Gino. Eager to dispel that impression, I sat up tall. "Making people see only sweetness is why I'm so good at my job." Still, my insides clenched, and the way things were going maybe it'd be wise for me to write my obituary. "Let's talk about it tomorrow, after you've slept."

I sighed, thinking there would be no sleep for me tonight.

I was right. I said goodnight to Michael, but when I got home, even after two drinks, instead of sleeping like Rip Van Winkle, my night consisted of tossing and turning. Frustrated, I pulled out my notes on Constance's life, what there was of them. She spent most of her time working as the manager in the Research and Development department at Triton Pharmaceuticals. Rose up pretty fast from a pharmacy technician position. Until her demise, four employees reported to her. Three women and one man. Guys don't always cotton to taking orders from a woman, so he required investigation. But what about her tossed office? Was someone looking for something or taking out their rage even further?

The next morning, I called Detective Corrigan to inform him Michael Adler was still my client on this case.

"Miss DeNardo, are you sure you want to do this?" His tone of voice made it clear he'd be happier if I ran the other way.

"Perfectly."

"I can't stop you, but make sure you share any

information with the police. Anything less could be construed as obstruction of justice."

My voice went up an octave. "Of course. But you must understand my job is to do what's best for my client." I squeezed my eyes shut, bracing myself for his comeback. To my relief, it was anticlimactic.

"As long as you don't get in our way."

I poured on the honey. "Understood." I was in it now up to my trembling knees.

While showering and dressing, I planned my day. First stop, Triton Pharmaceuticals to talk to Constance's staff.

My quest took longer than anticipated. The receptionist handed me a visitor pass and instructed me to wait for the human resources manager. Upon his arrival, Mr. Human Resources pushed his glasses up on his nose and cleared his throat. "You know, Ms. Adler's staff talked with the police earlier. Can't you just confer with the detective who came here and not bother our employees? Ms. Adler's death and all these subsequent questions are affecting everyone's productivity."

I wanted to bonk him on the head with his stapler. "Someone was murdered here and productivity is your main concern?" Continuing to lay it on thick, "Don't you feel just a little ashamed?" I planted my hands on my hips to emphasize the scolding.

He looked a little embarrassed so I went for the gold. "You allowed Detective Corrigan to ask questions, but you won't let me. Is it because I'm a woman and the detective was a man?" I picked the right way to go. No one in Human Resources wants to hear a cry of discrimination.

The first person he took me to see was Tara

Hamilton, the business development team leader whose career at Triton spanned almost twenty years. Longer than Constance's ten.

Maybe some jealousy? "Thank you for meeting with me, Ms. Hamilton."

She sniffed. "It's Mrs. and did I have a choice? Besides, I told everything I knew to the real police who were here before you."

I bristled at her comment but was determined not to be put off. "Yes, but perhaps, from one woman to another, you might now recall something you didn't mention."

It was like trying to get milk from a cactus. "No, there isn't. But I did leave out how loud the fight between Constance and Brody Eagleton from Research was that evening before she died. Not that I listened in. I'm not the kind of person who eavesdrops."

"You didn't overhear anything by accident?"

She didn't even consider the possibility. "No, of course not."

"How did Constance seem the next day?"

Mrs. Hamilton wrinkled her nose as if changing a nasty diaper. "Like always. As if the world belonged to her and she deserved it."

"Are you saying she was full of herself?"

"She never gave anyone else credit for their hard work. Plus, she could do no wrong. Nothing bad ever stuck to her."

It was clear Mrs. Hamilton resented Constance, but she didn't fit my idea of someone who'd commit this murder. "She acted like everything was fine?"

"As a matter of fact, she behaved downright cheerful. Knowing her, she had won whatever fight they had."

Did Eagleton come back the next night to claim his own victory? "Anything else, Mrs. Hamilton?"

Since she didn't add to that, I thanked her and she went on her way, no doubt believing she carried the fate of Triton on her shoulders.

The police began their investigation with Brody Eagleton, no doubt now a 'person of interest'; another name for 'Don't leave town or you're busted.' Since they had already interviewed him, it was tempting to postpone my meeting. Instead, I steeled myself for battle.

Talking to Eagleton was easier said than done. First, his administrative assistant had to be persuaded to give me an appointment. She eventually agreed to squeeze me in at 4:30, which gave me enough time to interview Constance's other staff members.

Nothing useful there except for a tidbit from the late Constance's last hire, Mallorie, who reminded me of one of those too-much-makeup mean girls featured on reality TV. The kind in high school who used to scare me whenever I spotted more than one of them together. Not only can packs be vicious, but I lived in fear of going blind from the combined fumes of their hair spray.

Mallorie claimed Constance and Brody Eagleton had something going on. Asked for details, though, she admitted she just felt a lot of 'chemistry' between them. I'd plug into Mallorie's supposed vibes in my meeting with Eagleton.

At 4:30 sharp, I stood outside his office while Eagleton talked with a younger duplicate of himself. Same meticulous, expensive clothing and same coiffed hair. Together, their ties probably cost the same as my living room sofa.

Eagleton wagged his finger at the other man, as if

emphasizing his own words. I imagined he was ordering the destruction of all evidence. Eagleton's briefcase sat open on top of his desk and while he continued to talk, he began stuffing it with papers. Not wanting this bird to fly away before we talked, I cleared my throat and stepped inside his office. "Mr. Eagleton, Claire DeNardo. I'm working with the police." Afraid he'd blow me off, I rushed my next words. "Just a few questions for you."

"I'll leave you two alone." The younger man retreated, looking relieved.

Eagleton turned on me, his brown eyes dark, his face twisted by rage. Without thinking, I retreated one step. So he couldn't see my hands trembling, I clasped them behind my back.

He slammed down the top of his briefcase.

I begged my legs not to collapse and held my breath, hoping he wouldn't leap over the desk and throttle me.

Instead, he ground his teeth. "Miss Whoever-the-Hell-You-Are..." I opened my mouth, but he waved my attempted response away. "You're misrepresenting yourself. You're a private investigator, and I have nothing to say to you."

My voice came back. "Mr. Eagleton." Gino told me to call someone by their name to help calm them. "I understand you've talked to the police. But sometimes, later on you remember a detail that clears everything up. That's why I'm here."

A vein in his temple throbbed. "You want something fresh? I'll tell you something. My wife just called. She wants a divorce. You see, the cops talked to her too."

My mouth went dry and my tongue felt like it would stick to the roof of my mouth, but I'd waited too long for this opportunity, so I continued treading on dangerous ground. "You were having an affair with Constance." My already racing heart sped up even more. I was scared of fainting before he replied.

He snorted. "That's ridiculous. Anyone would say she was an attractive woman. Powerful women often are. We worked together, sometimes long hours. But that was it." He growled. "Your associates, the cops, convinced my wife otherwise."

I didn't buy it, but there was no sense in riling him any further. "Okay, so what were you arguing about the evening before her death?"

He looked at me like he was a bull and I was a red cape. "I don't have to answer any more of your questions. If you're working with the police like you claim, they can fill you in." He grabbed his briefcase and reached for the door knob. "Now, if you'll excuse me, I have to try to put my life back together."

He left me standing alone in his office. My knees felt weak enough to buckle and I considered sitting in Eagleton's chair until they recovered. Then a better idea hit me, making me smile like my mother's old cat we called Shreddy.

I played with one of my earrings until it popped out and landed on Brody's desk. Then in a loud voice announced, "Oh my, my earring fell off." I rifled through the papers on his desk, hoping there'd be something of interest. Nothing.

If someone walks by, I'll claim my earring fell into one of his desk drawers. My ears tuned in for Brody's return while my brain screamed about my insanity. By the last drawer, my breaths were as ragged as if I'd run a marathon. Getting ready to zip out of there, I spotted a card with Constance's name preceded by "You amaze me." *Yes!* Footsteps growing closer stopped me from pulling it out of the drawer.

The exact truth was my whole body froze and didn't relax until the steps went in the opposite direction. I licked my lips, snatched the card, slipped it into my purse and slowly closed the drawer. Then as casually as possible took my leave from Eagleton's office.

I walked right into a well-dressed woman. Through clenched teeth she asked, "Where's my cheating, no-good husband? And who are you?"

My mind went blank with panic. "Oh, uh…" I stuck out my shaking hand. "Claire DeNardo, Mrs. Eagleton. I'm working with the police on—"

"That slut's murder." She spat. "The police have already asked me about my husband's involvement." She placed her hands on her hips. "I had no idea she was the reason for all his late nights." Her eyes narrowed. "Who did you say you were?"

"Claire DeNardo." She reminded me of my Uncle Carl's first wife, the mean-spirited Aunt Tina. I used to beg my mother not to leave me alone with her. I was sure the flying monkeys did her bidding. "My condolences you had to find out this way." Maybe I could get on her good side, if there was one. "Sometimes men who have it all still stray."

She waved off my comment. "Did he say where he was going?"

"Home."

"Probably to take my jewelry and hock it." She snarled and spun around on her expensive heels, probably to head him off at the pass.

As soon as Mrs. Eagleton was out of sight, I fled and didn't look back until reaching my car. I skimmed the card after smoothing it out on my leg, going through it once, then again, forcing myself to slow down to make sure something important didn't get past me.

I frowned and slapped my hand against the steering wheel. I'd risked my safety for nothing more incriminating than a note from Constance thanking Eagleton for the flowers he'd sent her. No mentioned appreciation of his sexual prowess or even having a 'wonderful night together.' Only a thank you for his thoughtfulness. Despite the note being a big disappointment, I decided to keep it. Maybe it would be a link to something more incriminating.

Preoccupied with the possibilities and paying no attention to my driving, I almost backed into a security guard on a Triton go-cart. The guard laid on his clown horn at the last minute. I mouthed an apology, thankful my car hadn't plowed into the guy.

I hadn't even driven to the end of the lot when an idea struck me hard, and I did a u-turn. That guard might have seen something last night. It was worth a chance, not that the cops wouldn't have already questioned him.

The cart was where it'd been, but no guard stood near. Maybe he'd be in the smoking area. Most security guards of my acquaintance killed time, smoking. This one may have seen who killed Constance.

Sure enough, I found him at the back of the building near a trashcan/ashtray. The name tag sewed on his uniform read, 'Ed'. He looked like one of the high school hoods-in-training who, if you were smart, you avoided at all costs. A wiry guy with slicked-back hair and tattoos on both of his sinewy arms, his face became even gaunter as he sucked a final draw on his cigarette, which he then flicked into the ashtray. "Hey, you're the one almost ran me over."

Without thinking, the sheepish, little-girl grin I always gave my father rolled across my face. "Sorry about that. Really. It's just I'm so preoccupied with poor Constance's death. Did you know her?" I held my breath, worried he'd tell me to get lost.

"Yeah. Who didn't?"

My tensed-up shoulders lowered. "She was friendly?"

He pulled a toothpick out of his pocket. "Not to the likes of me. Don't want to talk bad about the dead, but I seen her buttering up the bigwigs." He waved his toothpick around for emphasis. "After hours, know what I mean?"

"Besides Brody Eagleton?"

He snorted. "He was just a stepping stone."

"Have you talked to the police about what you've seen?"

The toothpick made it into the corner of his mouth. "Yeah, sure. Fat lotta difference it'll make."

"I don't follow you."

He hiked up his baggy pants. "Cops don't think of security guards as anything but cast-offs. So we play respectful, but it ain't what any of us feel."

It was obvious he didn't like the police. That could make it easier for me to get some information he didn't give up to them. Besides, this guy had underdog written all over him. I could identify with that. "Yeah, they don't always pick up on what a guy on the inside, like you, knows."

"Got that right. Take Miss Adler. Why'd anyone want her dead?"

Not knowing if it was a rhetorical question or not, I

waited.

He leaned on the wall with his foot flat against it. "Could be some folks think her latest lover got possessive. My money, though, is on a bigwig's missus."

"Really? Did you see something that night?" Had he noticed Eagleton's wife stomp out of the building after she'd confronted me?

"Nah. I'm just shootin' the breeze." He pitched the toothpick into the trashcan. "Anyway, I gotta go make my rounds." He ambled off.

I followed and handed him my business card. "If anything you think is important comes to mind, please call me."

He shot me a look that told me not to hold my breath. But he did take the card.

I got back in my car and called Michael. The picture he'd painted of Constance didn't match the one everyone else gave me. Either he didn't really know his sister or he'd purposely left out the more colorful aspects of her life. Which was which? I'd worked with untrustworthy clients before, but those were on he-said-she-said cheating spouse cases. Dishonesty was the basis for those situations. I had only taken on this case because Michael seemed so needy and alone. Now I realized he may not be what he appeared to be. Nor so alone. Lies about his sister could be keeping him company.

Needing to dig into the facts of the real Constance, I headed back to my office. My computer was firing up when my phone rang. I checked to see who it was, hoping the guard, Ed, had a revelation.

No such luck. It was my Aunt Lena. *Why now?*

"Claire, honey. Did you forget? You were supposed to come help me at the cafe. Your father's here, but he keeps trying to dip a spoon into the whipped cream. I can't hold him off forever."

I pushed my hair away from my forehead. "No, I didn't." *I did.* "I'm in the middle of a client's case but I can wrap it up and be there before you know it."

My aunt sighed. "Hurry. I need you here. We're crazy with customers." Her voice got louder, "Frank, put that spoon down."

Like the rest of the women in my family, my aunt thinks nothing of having two or three conversations at once, so before she got involved with my dad, I looked at my watch. "Give me twenty minutes." I hung up and frowned, realizing my miscalculation. It'd take me at least twenty-five minutes to get there.

All the way to my aunt's bakery, *Cannoli's*, I tried to fit everything about Constance's murder and what she was really like, together. It was a puzzle where you have the border pieces, but none of the inside ones. Impossible to make out the picture.

I drove past the bakery's front window and noticed my father standing there. No doubt assigned by Aunt Lena to watch for me.

Before I got through the restaurant's kitchen door, my aunt confronted me, waving a mixing paddle around. Dots of cream flew everywhere. "Your father's gonna eat me out of business."

I kissed her flushed cheek. "Sorry."

She sniffed, which meant I wasn't totally forgiven. "Everything's going crazy. Kiss your father hello, then take over at the counter."

I rang up enough cakes and pastries to give half of Ohio diabetes. My feet screamed for mercy. Aunt Lena was the official owner of *Cannoli's* but the whole family had agreed to pitch in while her niece Josie, daughter of her deceased husband's brother and her kitchen assistant, was nearing the end of her second pregnancy. A twinge of guilt plucked at my heart when I realized so far, my father had done most of the helping.

At long last, it was time to close up shop. Aunt Lena took off her apron and asked, "So who's the big client you couldn't interrupt to help your aunt?"

My dad jumped in. "Lena, she got here and worked hard. Leave it alone."

I swallowed the last bite of a small éclair that had teased me with its glorious ganache all evening. "The client needed some handholding, that's all."

My aunt squinted at me. "I hope that's all he held."

"Someone murdered his sister." I regretted the words as soon as they fell from my chocolate-tinged mouth.

My aunt sucked in a breath and my dad leaned in toward me. "Claire Marie." The last time he used my middle name was when I ran over a stop sign with his new car. "I never liked that private detective job for you. But this is too much. If someone hurt you, I'd have to kill them myself."

My aunt joined in. "Why can't you work here? There's plenty to do. You don't have to run around with some hoodlum."

I slumped against the glass case, realizing this battle had just begun. "He's not a hoodlum."

My aunt threw up her hands. "Frank, she's protecting a hoodlum."

I kept my voice steady and spoke slowly, telling myself it was like talking to people who were unfamiliar with the English language. "I'm helping the police here. Nothing more. End of story."

Aunt Lena sniffed and began to wipe down the counter. My dad started to clean off the tables. The sound of it all in a silent room was deafening. I laid my hand on top of my aunt's. "I promise I'm in no danger. I'm not his guard. More like a friend."

She looked at me, her eyes moist. "You know I worry. Since your mother died, I feel extra responsible for you." She placed both of her chunky hands over her heart and looked toward the ceiling. "Promised her I'd look after you." She wiped a drop of sweat from her upper lip. "How will I face her in heaven knowing, instead of settling down with a nice man, you're hanging around with no-goods."

I put my arms around her soft, ample middle. "I'm sure Mom thinks you've done a great job with me. And don't worry. Everything's fine."

She hugged me back, and then pushed me to arm's length. "Okay. But now don't do anything to embarrass the family."

I wanted to laugh. My family specialized in doing things to embarrass the rest of us. There was the time my tipsy Aunt Julia whipped off her wig and tossed it at the same time the bride tossed her bouquet; or when my cousin Tomasina tried to climb inside her ex-husband's coffin. It'd be hard to top times like those. "Aunt Lena, you have my assurance there's nothing I can do to embarrass this family."

Belly overfilled, I shuffled back to my car and chastised myself for gobbling that third éclair and, as with every other time I took a shift at the bakery, was thankful not to be working there full time. It was one of my biggest fears that my body would look like a meatball. Let's face it. Eating is a huge passion of mine.

Combine that with my fat-welcoming genes and I'm almost doomed to someday shop in the plus, plus-size section of Macy's.

After a satisfactory grieving time for needless calories, my mind moved on. There was a crime to solve. Tracking down Triton's security guard, Ed, again was the best way to work the case and burn some calories.

I yawned and checked the time and was surprised to see it was after 11:00 p.m. The only way to talk to Ed tonight was by waking him up. No, it'd be better to go home and hope to come up with what to do about Michael. Maybe my dreams would accomplish that.

There was enough time for me to slip into my jammies, but not enough to slip into dreamland, before my phone rang. It was Michael. A spark of dread ran down my spine. Knowing it couldn't be good, I still picked up the phone.

Chapter Three

His words rushed together. "Someone broke into my house. Every room is ripped apart."
The hairs on the back of my neck stood at attention. "Are you okay?"

"Just shaken up."

"Call the police. I'll be right there." I scrambled out of bed and threw on some clothes, all the while scolding myself for not seeing this coming. But then, the cops hadn't thought about it either.

The police got there first. I'd no sooner stepped through Michael's door when Detective 'Blue Eyes' Corrigan snarled, "Doing a bang-up job of working with the police, I see."

My eyes became saucers. To say I was blindsided was an understatement. "What do you mean?"

Corrigan waved a piece of paper under my nose. "Did you happen to see this?" Before any words managed to pass my lips, he leaned in so close I could smell his spicy cologne, and it was tempting to just close my eyes and inhale. His stern tone stopped me mid-breath. "It's evidence. You know what that is, don't you?"

My first impulse was to step back. Instead, I held my ground. It wouldn't look good for Michael's PI to weasel away. "Yes. Of course." I crossed my arms then remembered this gesture could be viewed as a sign of self-protection, and uncrossed them. No need to let Corrigan think he intimidated me, even if he did. "But I don't know what you're talking about."

"Sure you don't." He rapped the paper against the palm of his hand. "It happens to be a list of initials Constance Adler wrote down before she died. The funny thing is, we might never have seen it, if this break-in hadn't occurred."

"I've never seen that piece of paper before." It might have helped if Corrigan had let me read the list, but it was plain to see, cooperation wasn't on his mind. Maybe Michael could tell me the list's meaning after the police were gone. If he knew.

I made it a point to turn my back on Corrigan. After all, Michael's welfare was my job, not arguing with a detective carrying an attitude along with his badge.

Speaking of Michael, the poor guy sat in a chair in his torn-apart living room. His clothes were so wrinkled it was like he'd been knocked down and walked on. Angry shaving nicks covered his face. Only a fool would believe Michael was coping with his sister's murder. Everything about him shouted his misery. I fought the wild urge to cradle him like a little kid who's skinned his knee. I crouched down and kept my voice soft. "Michael, did you see anyone lurking around the house?"

He shook his head, his jaw clenched. But the look in his eyes surprised me. I expected fear, maybe shock, but his stony glare shouted angry-as-hell to me.

Corrigan tapped his foot. "We've already been through that."

I took a deep breath and waited. "Michael?"

Michael's legs bounced up and down and his hands clutched the armrests so tight his knuckles were white. "Didn't see anyone, but this had everything to do with Constance's murder."

Almost in unison, Detective Corrigan and I said, "We'll get whoever did this." For a second I thought we could continue working with that same cohesion and maybe even goodwill. But he destroyed that notion with his next words. "Of course, it would help if Ms. DeNardo kept us informed."

Trying my best to ignore Corrigan and his unhelpful comments, I asked Michael, "Do you want to spend the night here or go to a hotel? A hotel may be best, at least for tonight." Most people wouldn't be comfortable sleeping in a house right after someone had broken into it. A shiver ran through me at the thought of someone breaking into my home, maybe even going through my underwear drawer. I resolved to do laundry tomorrow.

"I'm staying."

Corrigan shook his head firmly. "Not a good idea. Whoever did this might return."

Michael's voice was controlled fury. "I'll be ready."

Whatever he had in mind couldn't be good. "You're angry and that's understandable. But sometimes it makes people do the wrong thing, make bad decisions."

Corrigan joined in. "She's right. Don't do anything stupid." With a sideways glance at me, he added, "And you, Ms. DeNardo, let me do my job."

I wanted to dig my heel into Corrigan's foot, but that'd just get me arrested for assault. "Come on,

Michael, I'll take you to the Marriott. You'll be safe there." I gave him a look I hoped he'd interpret as, "Just agree, so we can talk alone."

He turned toward the hallway. "I'll go grab a toothbrush."

After checking in at the hotel, Michael still looked jittery but telling him to relax would've sounded so callous. Instead, I allowed my mouth to operate before my brain knew and broke Gino's Rule Number Two: "Never drink with a client." This was different though. No hidden motives. I plastered on a smile as fake as my old neighbor's pink, plastic flamingos. "Let's get you a drink." Without waiting for an answer, I steered him toward the hotel's lounge.

The alcohol might have gotten him talking about Constance and that list Corrigan called me on. Of course, he would have needed to drink at least some of it. Instead, he stared down at his finger and ran it around the rim of his glass. On the other hand, I was so dry it felt like a cactus had taken root in my mouth. But it wouldn't look good for me to down a drink in a single gulp. Besides, I needed all my senses about me. Just one glass of wine on a practically empty stomach, and I'm doing karaoke even without a karaoke machine.

I pushed my hand against my stomach as it growled. It was now about breakfast time and we hated going hungry. "Sorry you're going through this, Michael, but there are some questions that need answering."

He removed his glasses and rubbed his eyes. The dark circles around them confirmed he hadn't slept much. He quickly slipped the glasses back on. "Don't be sorry. Anything to help." He took a sip.

It seemed so cold to forge ahead when he was in so

much pain, but what had transpired between Corrigan and him before I arrived was important. I downed a bit of my drink for courage. "What did the police ask you?"

Michael swallowed hard. "They wanted to know if she had kept any letters from…" He sighed deeply and his shoulders slumped. "Her lovers."

"Did she?" If so, the police or the killer surely had them by now.

"No." He hesitated. "She didn't keep any *letters*. A few days before she was killed, though, she made up a list with a bunch of initials."

"That's what Corrigan was waving around?"

He sighed. "I was going to show it to you, but then someone broke in." He spit the last words out. "Luckily I had it with me or whoever did it would've gotten the list for sure."

"Do you know what the initials stood for?"

"No, but some had checkmarks after them." He folded and unfolded his hands. "The letters 'BE' were on the first line."

I sat up straight. They had to stand for Brody Eagleton. "Do you remember any of the others?"

He rubbed his face hard. "The second initials were 'JL,' but that's all I remember." He dropped his hand away. I've seen mannequins looking more energized.

I wanted to throw my arms around him and comfort him. But hugs convey a number of things. They can mean, "It'll be all right," or "I understand" or even "You're not alone." I'd already broken two of Gino's rules so settled for a keeping-my-distance pat on his forearm. This relationship had to stay professional all the way to find out the truth about Constance and her death.

I skipped any sort of segue into the subject. "Michael,

it's pretty clear your sister wasn't exactly a nun."

The vein in his temple kept rhythm to a silent beat, and he frowned. "No, she wasn't. She was ambitious and did whatever it took to get ahead."

"She didn't just get on the bad side of one disgruntled employee did she? From what I heard she made a lot of enemies."

"Warned her someone would get hurt. Didn't know it'd be her."

"Did she talk about anyone in particular? Like Brody Eagleton?" I hated how hard this was on him, but he'd hired me to find Constance's killer. "Michael?"

"She planned to end it with him."

"When?"

He stared past me, toward the wall, looking like he wished he was anywhere but here. "She didn't say."

His dog-in-the-pound look stopped me. I couldn't drill him anymore tonight. "Come on, Michael. We'll talk more in the morning. Time for you to try and get some sleep."

He shook his head. "Not yet. It's my turn to apologize."

Difficult as it was, I didn't allow any emotion to show on my face. "For what?" *What did he do and how bad was it?*

"For not being totally honest."

My heart boomeranged in my chest. "Is it something else about Constance's list?"

He looked into his glass and shook his head. Seconds ticked by, but he didn't move. I'm not good at waiting games, but feared he'd spook if rushed.

At long last, he picked up his glass, drained it, and coughed. I perched on the edge of my seat, afraid I'd have to do CPR.

He hung his head and templed his fingers. “Worse.”

I’d only had a small bit of wine, but even that sloshed around in increasing waves. “Tell me.”

Chapter Four

His cheeks flushed and he kept his eyes on the table. “Constance was hurting herself and other people.” He paused again.

I sat motionless, like a priest waiting for a sinner to confess. “And?”

His shoulders hunched a bit. “I wrote those threatening letters.” His next words gushed out. “I thought it’d make her do the right thing.”

My head jerked. “What?” He had to be kidding. “You lied to me from the beginning? But why did you take one of the letters to the cops? What if they had investigated?” I slapped my hands down flat on the table. *What else wasn’t true?*

He looked away from me, his face red. “She didn’t take them seriously. Thought they were a prank. All three of them. I thought the police could convince her…” He put his head in his hands. “It was stupid. Guess I wasn’t thinking straight.”

I cupped my hands over my mouth and took a couple of deep breaths, trying to calm down. When that didn’t work I dropped my hands into my lap and spoke sharply.

"Why didn't you tell me that when you hired me?"

"I couldn't. You might not have taken the case. Then when Constance was killed..." He placed both his hands over mine and pleaded. "Don't think badly of me. I was only trying to keep my sister safe."

I slipped my hand from his and sat back, feeling slightly queasy. What if the cops discovered the truth about the letters? Michael might be arrested. Corrigan already believed I was withholding information. I pushed my hair back from my face and realized the necessity of my staying on the case just to have some control. "Okay, Michael, but tell me something. You showed me the first two letters. What happened to the third?"

He dropped his chin and mumbled into his chest. "She told me she'd ripped it up and tossed it out."

I could only hope she'd told him the truth and he wasn't lying to me. I gathered my things to leave. "Okay, we'll figure out what to tell the police tomorrow. It's late. Try to get some sleep." My chest felt heavy, sort of like when I learned Santa Claus wasn't real. I should have known Michael, the good guy, wasn't totally real either.

***

It never fails. I wash my face, brush my teeth, and fall into bed, only to lie awake. My thoughts about Michael falsifying evidence ran wild. *Would they arrest him?* I worried that scenario to death. Next on the agenda, a good case of regret. *Why had I gotten myself involved in this mess?* To top it all off, I really didn't look forward to finding Ed again. He made me uneasy. Like the boys in high school who were constantly in detention, or suspended so many times, they didn't graduate until they turned twenty.

My mantra, *I can handle it. I am woman, hear me roar,* didn't help since to my mind, it sounded more like mewing, I had to repeat the phrase about twenty times before falling asleep.

The next morning, I grabbed three chocolate-covered caramel-and-nut squares and threw them in a plastic bag. They'd be my reward for getting through the day.

First up, a call to Michael while I sat in traffic. I was hoping he hadn't done something dumb like talk to Detective Corrigan. According to Gino, too much honesty is never a good thing. His code was "truth in moderation." In this case, Michael needed to heed that bit of wisdom.

He didn't answer, so I left a message for him to call me back as soon as possible.

Ed was next on my list. I pulled into Triton's parking lot and scanned the area without luck. Once inside, Triton's receptionist informed me Ed came on at two in the afternoon. Rather than return to my office to catch up on another client, I decided to visit Michael at the hotel, only to discover he'd checked out.

My fingers tapped a worried beat on my steering wheel as I debated going to the police station. But if Michael had gone there to confess he'd written those letters, he'd need a lawyer, not a private investigator. I could have kicked myself for not telling him that last night, but I had been too rattled. The thought of him in handcuffs stole my breath. He might be in big trouble, all because I hadn't thought fast enough.

The sunny side of my brain offered a better scenario. Maybe, just maybe, he went back home. I gunned the motor, whispering, "Please, please, please be there." As if my after-the-fact pleading would make a difference.

I rapped on Michael's door, my heart pounding. When he cracked it open, the scent of pumpkin mixed with cinnamon danced into my nostrils. My stomach immediately yearned to be close to the smell's origin.

Michael opened the door wider. "Sorry I didn't return your call. Just needed time to think." His voice was Prozac calm. Maybe he'd come up with a plan.

"I was worried sick." *Oh, God. That sounded more like my aunt than like a PI.* "I thought you might've gone to the police."

He took his glasses off and cleaned them on his shirttail. "I wouldn't do that without talking to you."

"That's good." I waited to see what he'd say next, but he didn't respond. "What're you going to do?"

He cleared his throat. "Right now, have breakfast. If you're hungry, why don't you join me?"

My stomach growled a mating call to whatever he was cooking. "I am, a little." Gino probably had a rule about never eating something a client made. In case Gino did, I added, "I'd like to watch you cook. Then we can discuss how to handle that letter issue while we eat."

He ushered me into his kitchen, past the still-tumbled rooms. "Too late. Breakfast is ready. Pumpkin pancakes with cinnamon whipped cream sound good?"

I nodded my head and smiled. "Very good."

Michael plated two pancakes, doused them with real whipped cream and placed them before me with a dazzling flourish. He watched as I cut into the fluffy masterpieces. My tastebuds purred. "These are delicious."

He puffed out his chest and grinned. He looked younger and appealing, in that kid- with-a-great-science-project sort of way.

To mask my staring at him, I shoveled in a piece of pancake too big for my mouth and probably resembled a dog carrying a chew toy. As delicately as possible, I used my pinkie to guide the ends into my mouth, swallowing hard and praying the food would go down without a fight. Tears sprang to my eyes with the effort. He rushed to get me some water, which I gulped anxiously. "Thanks" came out as a croak.

My near-fatal pancake episode brought me back to reality. No more checking Michael out as if we'd met through an online dating service. This was business and I needed to treat it that way.

As tempting as it was to finish eating every last creamy bite, I pushed the plate away and reclaimed my PI voice. "Have you decided what you'll do with those letters?" Not that I really wanted to know. In fact, forgetting his confession overwhelmingly appealed to me, but my brain would have none of that.

"Already called my lawyer and left a message. She helped me before, when my business sold." He ran his hand through his thinning hair. "You have to believe me. Dragging you into my troubles wasn't part of the plan. Nor was getting you arrested along with me." He popped out of his chair and began to clear the table.

"It'll be okay." For his sake, I hoped my words sounded convincing. For my own sake, too. Having seen those mid-century women-in-prison movies, I sure didn't want to star in one.

His phone rang. It was his lawyer. Sitting at the edge of my chair, I listened to his end of the conversation which, after he explained the situation to her, consisted mostly of "uh huh."

When the call ended, I sat back, still tense. "Well?"

"She wants to see me at 1:00 this afternoon. Doesn't want me to talk to anyone about the issue until I get together with her."

"Is she aware I know about it?"

He shook his head. "Not yet."

Although silence enveloped us, my mind was anything but quiet. Would his attorney advise him to turn himself in?

I pulled my focus back to what I knew for certain. "In the meantime, a murderer is still out there." Needing to go yet not wanting to appear rude I asked, "Do you need help cleaning up in here or in the other rooms?" My mother would've been so proud. At the same time, Gino would be cringing.

"No. It's okay."

He walked me to the door. "You're a great cook, Michael."

"Thanks. It relaxes me."

In spite of Gino's rules, I liked this man. My stomach told me it wanted to be invited the next time he relaxed.

As soon as I left his home, my determination to discover the owner of the initials, JL, came back strong. My mission took a detour, though, upon my return to my office. Maria Waldini, who suspected her husband, Dominic, of cheating on her, had left five messages. They've been married 65 years, but she still wanted me to tail him. It was a relief for me to find he went to the park, played bocce ball, and met a few war buddies for a drink. Afterwards he returned home.

I called Maria back and gave her the report. Pitiful though my finances were, I informed her she'd get a full refund. She blessed me in enthusiastic but broken English, and Italian.

Warmed by her appreciation, I began my research on Brody Eagleton, Constance's final lover.

My findings included Brody's status as an only child born into an influential and wealthy family. The woman I'd met was the second Mrs. Eagleton, and they'd been married five years. His first wife left him, claiming spousal abuse. No arrests, but if he really had used his fists on his first wife, who was to say he didn't on Constance? His temper could have gotten out of hand and he could have pushed her hard enough. Then when he realized she was dead, he tossed her office to confuse the cops.

There was a bit more on the internet about Eagleton's family, but nothing worth noting. I shut my computer down, knowing some pavement pounding came next, but it was only 1:15. Michael would still be with his attorney. Maybe it'd be possible to see Ed at Triton before his shift began. Heading out the door, I then turned around and grabbed the chocolates I'd brought earlier. I needed psychological fortification to deal with Ed and, to me, nothing says happy time like chocolate oozing with caramel and nuts.

Ed was in the same spot as the first time we'd talked, leaning against the building, puffing on a cigarette. I bit into the last of my chocolate pieces and debated how to approach him, scratching off, "Don't you know cigarettes can kill you? Speaking of killing..."

I took a deep breath and vowed not to let this guy unnerve me. My knees didn't get the message because they wobbled. Terrified of falling at Ed's feet, I stopped a bit short.

I tried to sound casual. "Hey, Ed! You remember me, don't you?"

He glanced over at me with heavy-lidded eyes. "Sure, I remember you." He took a deep drag on his cigarette. "What d'ya want?"

I hesitated, as if he might bite me. "To ask you a few questions."

"Yeah?" He lifted his hand to eye level and stared at the cigarette's burning ashes. "First, it was the cops buzzing around and now it's you."

I pasted a smile on my face, but dropped it. Charming is not the word to describe me when I'm nervous. Empathy might work better. "Must be hard to do your job with cops asking questions all the time."

He snorted. "That ain't the problem." He picked a bit of tobacco from his tongue. "Problem is, no one's asking the right people the right questions."

I took a baby step toward him. "Enlighten me."

He took a final drag on his cigarette and crushed the butt with his shoe. "Gotta go. Shift's starting."

I piped up with something clever to delay him. "Wait."

He leaned back against the building. "Don't wanna stay a security guard forever, you know." His eyes ran up and down me. "Looks like you're doing all right."

What was he getting at? He couldn't possibly want to work for me. The pancakes in my stomach flipped, but if it could help Michael in any way, it would be best to play along. I raised an eyebrow and kept my voice level. "Are you looking for a job?"

He smiled, showing his tobacco-stained teeth. "You offering?"

My mouth went dry, but instead of screaming, "Are you nuts?" I managed to keep calm. "Depends. What've you got?"

He stared off toward Triton's brick and glass entrance. "Maybe I seen more than I told."

In movies, the PI slams the would-be stoolie against the wall and threatens him with injury if he doesn't cough up information. I just rubbed my forehead. "So you're holding out and letting a murderer run loose?"

He chewed on a cuticle. "Didn't say that." He folded his hands across his somewhat concave stomach. "All I'm saying is, I might could help you, under the right circumstances."

"Look, my business can't even afford me." Hiring him sure wasn't in my best interest, but if he knew more, I had to get it from him. "Maybe we can, you know, make an arrangement."

He gave me a crooked smile and rubbed his thumb against the tips of his fingers. "How about a green Benjamin?"

I jerked hard enough to make my neck hurt. "Fifty dollars?" It felt like my blood had been suddenly drained from me. "All I have is…" I pulled out my wallet. "Four Washingtons." How pathetic was that, waving those crumpled dollar bills in front of him.

He wasn't insulted enough not to snatch them and stuff them in his pocket.

I narrowed my eyes and talked out of the side of my mouth, like I'd seen in old movies. "Now, spill it."

He let out a short, harsh laugh. "Can't believe I'm giving you anything for four measly bucks." He rubbed his chin. "All right. You look like one of them honest girls. I can tell the good ones from the bitches. So we'll consider this a down payment. You know, information on the layaway plan."

I nodded like one of those bobble heads. "Agreed."

And wondered if it was possible to borrow money from my father.

Ed scanned the area, leaned closer and in a low voice said, "Eagleton wasn't the only hound on her trail." He paused. "John Luther, Eagleton's boss, was sniffing around her too."

My eyebrows shot up. Constance's list included the initials "JL" but no checkmark after them. "Was she interested?"

He snorted. "Her kind always goes after the power, and no one has more at Triton than Luther. His daddy started this company and he steps down the end of this year." Ed glanced at his watch. "Nothing like having a new woman when Sonny Boy takes over the throne." He took a few lazy steps toward Triton's entrance. Then he turned back around. "That's it for the $4. You want more, you gotta dish out more."

He walked off and raised his hand in a way I chose to interpret as a goodbye.

Undeterred, I shouted, "I'll be back." Sure he could no longer see me, I jammed my wallet back into my purse, slung the bag over my shoulder and stomped off. Some PI I was. Couldn't even afford an informant.

It didn't take long for my outlook to brighten though. Now I had John Luther's name and could check him out, even though Brody Eagleton continued to have my vote for Constance's killer. That led me to thinking. I was already at Triton so popping in on my favorite person of interest again seemed like a good idea. Remembering his bad temper and possible history of abuse, I reached in my purse for my pepper spray, ignored my racing pulse, and marched into Triton Pharmaceuticals.

Chapter Five

The receptionist politely reminded me, to enter the hallowed Triton halls, my visit had to be registered and an employee had to accompany me. Corporate privacy and all. I just as politely signed in and asked to be escorted to Brody Eagleton's office. I took a seat in the lobby, flipping through the pharmaceutical magazines they laid out to bore people as they waited. I guess there's a reason they never made a TV series about a pharmacist.

After forty-six minutes, I had checked my voicemail three times, filed a jagged fingernail, and debated asking for the restroom's location, when a man in a lab coat strode toward me. "Are you Miss DeNardo?"

I'm good at remembering faces and was pretty sure this was the guy who had been in Eagleton's office. I stood and nodded.

"Sean Lawrence, Drug Research Director. I work for Mr. Eagleton. Come with me, please."

Having a second crack at the hot-headed executive encouraged me until the memory of his temper came back. I glanced at Sean, who was about thirty and, despite that loose-fitting lab coat, looked to be in good shape. Maybe he'd intervene if his boss took a swing at me.

Unaware of my worries about obliteration by his boss, Sean said, "Mr. Eagleton is willing to see you, but he's very busy." He halted and looked straight at me. "Please understand, he's under a lot of stress. Don't make it worse."

For him or me? My fears hid behind a smiling mask. "I'm all about cooperation."

He gave me a quizzical look and said nothing. Once we turned down a long, empty hallway his tone turned conversational. "You're the first female private investigator I've met." He smiled. "Actually, the only private investigator I've ever met."

"You've probably never had any cause to see one."

He let out a warm chuckle. "I manage to stay on the straight and narrow."

After a maze of hallways, we finally arrived at Eagleton's office. Sean announced my presence and gave me a look that had 'good luck' written all over it. He closed the office door behind him.

I quickly shifted my focus to Battleship Eagleton, expecting all guns loaded, but he looked a lot more composed than during our last visit. Since he hadn't been arrested, he must have come up with a foolproof alibi.

I cleared my throat. "Thank you for seeing me, Mr. Eagleton. I just need clarification on some information."

He looked at me like I was a lemon he had to suck on. "I agreed to see you to clear the air. Once I do that, you'll leave me alone?"

That was as likely as a rabbit using birth control. "May I sit down?" I was scared he'd hear my knees knocking.

"You won't be here long enough for that."

I shifted my weight from one foot to the other, wishing I hadn't worn heels today. "Earlier, you denied ever being involved with Constance." He stiffened. "But now you've as good as admitted it." I pressed my point hard. "Tell me, how angry were you when Constance told you she was ending the affair?"

He leaned back in his chair and waved his hand. "Actually, I was relieved. She was proving to be too high-maintenance for me."

"In other words you didn't mind she was leaving you for another, more successful man."

He templed his hands. "If that comment was meant to provoke me, it's not working. It was obvious how she planned to climb the corporate ladder." He smirked like he'd just told a nun a dirty joke. "Her body was her biggest asset and sex her most utilized skill set."

That wasn't the reaction I'd expected. So far, he'd kept his responses cool, with well-rehearsed lines. Still, I'd have felt a lot safer holding one of those riot shields in front of me. "So you're implying that when you were arguing with her right before she was killed, it wasn't about being dumped?"

The vein in his temple kept time with my racing heart. "That's ridiculous. Of course it wasn't."

"Then what was it about?"

"Strictly business, like I told the police. She missed an important filing deadline for a new drug. Her delay could end up costing Triton millions."

"Since she worked for you, did you get in trouble?"

"What are you driving at?"

"First she drops you. Then she makes you look bad.

You must've been furious."

He stood up, and his voice was a low rumble. "You've asked enough questions."

I wanted answers and my words rushed out. "It wouldn't be the first time you hit a woman, would it?"

He charged at me, his eyes slits, fists clenched. "Who the hell do you think you are? I ought to—"

A loud knock on the door interrupted and a voice sounding like dry leaves on fire came through. "There a problem in there?" Ed cracked open the door and stuck his head in.

Eagleton ran his finger inside his shirt collar and cleared his throat. "No, Ed. No problem. I was just about to escort Miss DeNardo out."

My shoulders lowered, and my feet finally unglued themselves from the floor. My eyes never left Eagleton. "Since you're here, Ed, you can walk me out instead."

My now-favorite guard nodded. "Sure thing."

Ed waited until we were outside the building to scowl. "Didn't peg you for a tough broad, but I figured you for a smarter one. If you don't watch yourself, you could be the next corpse."

I exhaled loudly, trying to blow off some tension. "There were plenty of people in the office, and I would've screamed."

"Didn't you notice? It's quittin' time. That office was as deserted as a club with an eighty-year-old stripper."

He was right. I'd been foolish, taken an unnecessary risk. "Thank you."

He waved my thanks away. "Hate to see a little thing like you get hurt." He gave a short nod and half-smiled. "Besides, I'm protecting my investment."

My eyebrows disappeared into my hairline.

"Investment?"

"Yeah. You know, you pay me, I offer information and," he shrugged. "Protection."

I put my hands on my hips. "Wait a minute. I didn't ask you to barge in there."

He snorted and his nostrils flared. He needed his nose hairs trimmed. "Yeah, you'd rather have been dead meat."

I held up my hand. "Of course not."

He looped his thumbs through his belt, and his tone turned philosophical. "Look you need me, you know, to feed you info and protect you in tight spots. So what if you can't afford me right now? What's this case gonna pay you? Ten, fifteen grand? I can wait."

I almost laughed out loud. My cases never paid anything like that. Ten thousand or so described my total income for the year. As far as Ed went, there was another concern. He had 'drifter' written all over him. Not exactly the type to have to depend on.

"Think about it. But don't take too long." His granite expression softened slightly. "Hate to see someone nice like you get hurt." He pulled a toothpick from his pocket and lodged it in his mouth. "Gotta go." He sauntered off like a weary sheriff going to collect the town drunk.

I stood there, trying to think up a snappy response that never came. My phone rang, saving me from my humiliating silence.

"Claire?"

My stress eased just a bit when I heard the familiar voice. "Michael. What's going on?"

"Just left the lawyer's. She advised me—"

"Stop. Let's have this conversation at my office. How soon can you get there?" Maybe nobody was listening in on our conversation, but why take unnecessary chances. Maybe that should've been another of Gino's rules. "It pays to be paranoid."

By the time I got to my office, Michael was already there, pacing back and forth and wringing his hands. My brain buzzed, formulating an argument in case his lawyer wanted him to confess how he'd written those letters to Constance. He was too good of a guy to be put behind bars. Besides, maybe the only thing I wanted to see him behind was an oven, making me dinner.

"Stop it." I scolded myself. "He's a client, not your personal chef." Anyway, Gino probably had another rule about liking a client's cooking too much.

"Claire." Michael's face lit up like he was holding a winning lottery ticket.

"Let's go inside." I was so on edge I dropped the key and hit my head on the doorknob trying to pick it up. *Smooth, real smooth.* Thankfully I managed to unlock the door without giving myself a concussion.

As soon as the door closed behind us, I asked, my voice barely above a whisper, "What'd she tell you to do?"

"Keep it under my hat. She said to let the police discover it on their own."

I tilted my head, confused. "She wants the cops to figure it out?"

"No. She thinks it'll probably be a non-issue."

"Your lawyer actually thinks they'll just—" I tapped my forehead with the palm of my hand. "Forget about the letters?"

He shrugged. "She thinks I could become the primary suspect if they found out the truth now. I found my sister's body, remember?"

"Of course I remember," Snapping at him wasn't helping the situation, but I didn't have a good feeling about this. "What did you do with the letters?"

"She told me not to destroy them. So I put them in a bag of frozen lima beans."

I bit my lower lip. "Okay. We'll consider that problem on ice for now."

He smirked at my lame joke and we both took a seat, me behind my desk and him in the client chair to keep a professional distance between us. I described my encounter with Eagleton and filled him in about Luther's interest in Constance. Ed's help, I kept to myself, though. Clients should always believe their PI can handle the case without outside help. A PI has to keep her professional pride, not to mention her business.

When I finished, Michael slumped in his chair with his hand shading his eyes. "Constance couldn't have realized how dangerous her lifestyle was. If she had, she'd never..."

Good thing the desk was too big to reach over. I twitched, wanting to give him a thoroughly unbusinesslike hug, but settled for saying, "No matter how she lived, she didn't deserve to be murdered."

He nodded, but didn't look up.

In a bravado voice, I assured him, "We'll find the killer. They always make a mistake." I wanted to rewind and take those words back into my mouth. In the movies and on TV, killers make revealing errors, but how often did that happen in real life? I don't think he believed me anyway since he sat there, eyes still covered.

The awkward silence was broken by my cell phone chiming the Tarantella. "I better take this."

"Claire, honey, it's your Auntie Lena. How are you?"

I shut my eyes. The woman had the worst timing. "Fine. What's up?" I could picture her, covered with flour, her hairnet fighting to keep her curly hair from breaking sanitary rules.

"Need some help again. Your father was supposed to come in at four, but he's complaining about his lumbago."

Interrupting this case to serve pastries wasn't a great idea, but I hated shirking my responsibilities to the family my decision came quickly. "Okay, be there right away, but somebody's coming with me."

"A boyfriend? Is he Italian?" She was probably already pulling out the recipe for my wedding cake.

"No, on both counts."

"It's not that hoodlum you're protecting."

"No again. A friend." I wove a story. "We've been talking and it turns out, he likes to cook and would love to talk to you about pastries." I held my breath, waiting for either Michael or my aunt to protest.

Michael lifted his head and listened to my end of the conversation.

"Okay, bring him along." She sighed. "Are you sure there's nothing between you two?"

"No. Not possible." *At least not now.*

"He thinks he's too good for you?"

"No, that's not it." Before she could ask more questions, I ended her inquiry with, "See you soon."

Next up was convincing Michael it was good therapy. "We're going to my Aunt Lena's bakery. She's like you, loves to bake. It'll get your mind off Constance for a bit." I could hear Gino scolding me, "Never, never introduce a client to your family." He was probably turning over on his beach blanket about now.

As soon as we pulled around the back of *Cannoli's,* my sensible inner voice niggled at me that maybe this wasn't such a hot idea. I ignored it. Out loud, I assured a reluctant Michael, "You'll like my Aunt Lena. Besides being a wonderful baker, she's got such a good heart."

My aunt stood in the doorway, arms folded across her chest, feet spread apart as if ready for battle. She looked more like someone who'd eat your heart. It was obvious she didn't intend to make it comfortable for me and Michael, my non-Italian, non-boyfriend.

After I made the introductions, Aunt Lena sized Michael up with her dark, heavy-lidded eyes. "So, how long have you known my niece?"

Michael opened his mouth to respond, but I was faster. "For a while now." I grabbed two of the white aprons hanging from a hook, wrapped myself in one, and handed him the other. "I'll work the counter after bussing the tables. Michael, will you help?"

Without skipping a beat, he looked from me to Aunt Lena. "Is that okay with you, Mrs. Antonucci?"

She squinted at both of us and wiped her forehead with the back of her hand. "Are you sure—"

Before she could finish her thought, I exclaimed, "Oh, our first evening customer is here. Let's go, Michael." I grabbed his hand and yanked him through the door into the eating section.

With a steady supply of customers, I didn't have time to club myself for bringing Michael here. But I did have time to rationalize that he did need cheering up and as far as I knew, nothing says, "Happy Times" like a chocolate éclair, or a cannoli, crisp and bulging with creamy ricotta.

About thirty minutes later, Aunt Lena, displaying a

look of determination I imagine reporters wear when they're scooping a story, crooked her finger at Michael. His eyes pleaded with me, but I was in the middle of dealing with a customer who expected me to recite the virtues of a custard cake slice over a chocolate-dipped cream puff.

My throat constricted as Michael headed toward the swinging door and my aunt. The customer finally made her choice. Before she could change her mind, I plated the pastry and quickly slid the dish to her. The dollar bills stuck to my clammy hands and made it difficult to release the change. The tinkle of the coins she dropped in the tip jar echoed in my ears as I dashed into the kitchen, scared of what I'd find.

I skidded to a stop. Michael and Aunt Lena were hunched over a piece of paper, lost in deep, hushed conversation. *What now?* She was probably demanding he sign a contract agreeing to date me. I hustled over to break it up.

"Right here, it says to use walnuts." My aunt poked the paper with her chubby finger.

"I know, but if you try it with—" He spotted me and smiled. "We were discussing the best way to make her Midnight Tunnel cake."

Aunt Lena put her hands on her hips. "Your Michael thinks he knows a thing or two about baking."

I balked at her calling him mine but didn't correct her. "He does make good pancakes." My tongue should've slapped my lips for saying that.

Aunt Lena's eyes opened so wide I thought her eyeballs would pop out. "As in, he made you *breakfast*?"

I knew where her mind was and started to protest, but Michael cut me short. "Claire dropped by while I was making pancakes and I invited her to join me."

My aunt's eyes returned to normal size as they shifted from Michael to me. She threw up her hands. "It's not my business, but your mother would've wanted me to ask."

I didn't want to give my aunt an opening to probe further so simply said, "I better get back." Good thing, too, since three sugar-fix-seeking customers were waiting for me.

I muttered to myself while ringing up the bill for the three women. "Not what she thinks."

One of the ladies, her hand out for her change, asked, "Pardon?"

"Nothing. Really." I had to get a grip.

There was a lull in customer traffic and I took the opportunity to stare at the door that swung into the kitchen. Michael still hadn't returned to the dining room, and no talking sounds could be heard through the door. I turned, poised to put a stop to whatever my aunt was hatching. But my phone rang. It was Detective Corrigan. I wrinkled my nose and wondered if he smelled anything suspicious, like frozen lima beans.

"This is Claire. Hello, Detective Corrigan." My apron strings suddenly seemed like a noose around my neck.

Corrigan's voice boomed. "Miss DeNardo."

I held the phone away from my ear, worried he might bust my eardrum. "What can I do for you?" I tried to keep my tone light, but it's tough to sound pleasant while harboring a secret that could land Michael, and maybe even me, in jail.

"Heard you visited Eagleton. *Again.* Why?"

Two teenagers came in, chattering. I nodded to them, and then turned away. This was more important. Plus, I didn't want Corrigan to know Michael's hardboiled private detective also worked for her aunt behind a pastry counter. "Isn't he still a suspect?"

"That's not an answer."

One of the girls tapped on the glass counter. "Excuse me, ma'am. We want to order."

I held up my index finger and mouthed, "Give me a minute."

I pictured Corrigan arresting me while I doled out chocolate cupcakes. It wasn't a pretty picture. "Look, I was in the neighborhood and stopped by. Eagleton agreed to see me, and we talked. That's all there was to it."

"Talked? About what? Couldn't have been the weather."

"No." I paused to think. "He told me he had nothing to say. He just kept repeating that he was innocent. Then he had me escorted out." Although it sounded pretty lame, it was the truth.

"That's it? You're sure?"

"Of course I'm sure. Why? Are you going to arrest him?"

Corrigan probably had a scowl on his face. "We can't hold anyone without some solid evidence." He waited, like he was giving me an opening to confess to something.

Like most people, I hate silences and usually blurt out stupid, revealing things just to fill them. But I couldn't afford to do that this time, so my lips remained glued.

It worked. He talked first. "I'm going to repeat this once more. If you learn anything, you get in touch with me. Is that clear?"

So far, the only thing I'd learned was that Eagleton was an utter sleaze, Michael liked to cook, and he hid evidence in his freezer. But telling Corrigan all that would just anger him more, if that was possible, so I kept my response brief. "Crystal clear." I hung up and turned back to my teen customers.

Another fifteen minutes passed and my worry about what Aunt Lena might be putting Michael through grew, so I retreated to the kitchen before another customer appeared at the counter. Tiptoeing in, I spotted them leaning over the counter, side-by-side, elbows deep in flour and cocoa. They both appeared so happy. Before they noticed me, I sneaked back out. However much it thrilled me to see my aunt and Michael enjoying themselves, my brain kept reminding me Michael was a client.

He shouldn't be here with Aunt Lena and me. It was reckless and stupid to bring him along, not to mention shortsighted. It wouldn't pay for anyone in my family to develop a relationship with him, including me. I should have gotten that tattooed on my forearm.

A steady flow of customers kept me busy the rest of the evening. After the last one departed, Aunt Lena marched out of the kitchen, her face glowing with triumph. She carried a luscious-looking cake, crowned with fresh cherries, chocolate dripping down its sides. She carefully placed it on the glass counter and beamed. She tilted her chin toward Michael, who idled beside her. "This is Michael's creation. Can you believe this guy?"

He blushed. "I just helped."

I smiled, in spite of my worries about mixing business and family. "It looks delicious."

Aunt Lena glared at me like I'd said something

outrageous. “Are you kidding me? It’s a masterpiece. And we’re all going to have some.”

My fear of getting bigger hips forced me to say, “Just a forkful for me.”

My aunt snorted and cut a healthy piece for each of us. It was heaven on a plate.

After we’d each devoured our piece and Michael excused himself to wash up, my aunt confided, “I like your friend, Claire. He’s kind of cute without those glasses, and the man sure knows his way around food. That’s never a bad thing.”

Out of the corner of my mouth I said, “Forget it. It’ll never happen.”

She put her fluttering hand to her chest, a full-figured Italian Scarlett O’Hara. “Why, whatever do you mean?”

When Michael returned from washing his hands, I hurried the goodbyes and got him out of *Cannoli’s* before my aunt promised him my hand in marriage. It hadn’t been a good idea to bring Michael there, trusting him that much. Bad enough I liked him more than was practical. Even worse, I knew Aunt Lena now considered him a potential family member.

As we drove back to my office, Michael must have picked up on my signals. He cleared his throat and staring straight ahead, asked, “Is something wrong?”

His concern amplified my guilty feelings. I didn’t want the poor guy to feel bad. He’d been great in an awkward situation. “Of course not, everything’s fine. No problem here. Really, I mean it.” Even to me, my words sounded tight as the strings on a cello. So much for assuring him.

But it must have. In a lighter tone, he said, “I really liked your aunt.”

"She liked you too." I changed the subject. "Look, I've got some work to do. I'll drop you off."

His eyebrows rose in surprise, but he agreed.

Alone again, I dug up everything available on John Luther, heir to Triton Pharmaceuticals. His life had two themes. Privilege and wealth. Best schools, married to a beautiful socialite since his college days. Two handsome boys, both gainfully employed. No scandals. A big fat zero, which is how, at that time, I felt.

Sometimes it crosses my mind that a client could think I'm incompetent, but this time it worried me almost to the point of losing my appetite. Not only did Michael deserve the best; he had to believe he was receiving it too. I couldn't do this alone. So I chewed on a torn cuticle and weighed the pros and cons of asking Ed for his help. Inability to pay him weighed in quite heavily. Unless he let me pay him using a deferred payment plan. He'd joked about it, but he might agree to do it after all. I rubbed my forehead. If not, there were always my feminine wiles. In other words, I didn't have a chance.

Chapter Six

The next morning, pulling into Triton's parking lot, my chest felt like someone was standing on it, making it hard to breathe. I scanned the area but didn't see Ed, which added dismay to my anxiety. A rah-rah talk on my lips, I opened my car door and swung my legs out. A wolf whistle loud enough to pierce my eardrum made me jerk my head to see where it came from.

Ed had sneaked up by my car's back bumper. *So much for my powers of observation.* A smile blew across his face. "Figured you'd be back. Just not this soon."

My eyebrows knit as I thought hard, but no witty comeback flashed through my mind. "Yeah, well. I'm giving you a second chance."

He squinted. "Second chance?"

"To do the right thing."

He crossed his arms and the tattoo of a woman on his forearm danced. "You mean tell you everything I know, plus maybe do some snooping, for nothing." He shook his head and gave me a crooked grin. "Gotta admit, you got some cojones, but nothing worth anything is free."

"Okay." I rubbed my knuckles hard, like my

grandfather did when he was thinking. "How about I employ you," adding quickly, "for this case only."

Ed shaded his eyes from the sun. "For how much?"

"Five dollars per bit of information?"

He didn't have to say anything. His expression told me, "Kiss off." Loud and clear.

I sighed. Bargaining with money I didn't have scared me. Good thing debtors' prisons didn't exist anymore. "How about ten?"

He laughed. "That a joke?"

I held my purse closer to my body, like he'd swipe it from me. "No. It's what I can afford."

He stuck a toothpick in his mouth. The man must have been personally responsible for destroying a forest. "Twenty, and it's a deal. In fact, I have something for you already. Something I didn't tell you yesterday."

I wanted the information, but couldn't imagine how to pay for it. "$17.95."

He shook his head and rolled his toothpick to the other corner of his mouth. "This ain't an auction. Twenty."

I took the deal before he walked away. I wrinkled my nose, knowing ramen noodles were in my dining future. "Okay. Tell me what you know."

He held his hand out. "Money first. I figure you brought more than yesterday."

I nervously fingered the zipper on my purse. "Not exactly. Couldn't we do this on the layaway plan?"

He removed the toothpick from his mouth. "You didn't think I was serious."

"Why not? Layaway means I pay you a small advance, you know, to show good faith." He didn't object yet. "Once the case is solved, you'd get the rest of your money…" My voice got smaller as his frown grew bigger.

"What kinda idiot do you take me for?"

"No kind. I just can't afford to pay you today. Or tomorrow." Convinced he'd tell me to go away, I opened my car door.

He shut it before I could get in, threw down the toothpick and leaned against my car. "I'll do it. My ole ma always told me to give to charity." He rubbed his face hard. "And kiddo, you're the neediest case I ever seen."

I inwardly cringed and handed Ed my last wrinkled and tattered ten dollar bill.

He unfolded it and smoothed it out, like he held a treasure map. He then stuck it in his back pocket. "Two days before she died, John Luther dropped the late Ms. Adler off at work. From the looks of them, they weren't just carpooling."

"You'd think they would've been more discreet."

He shrugged. "It was too early for most folks to be here." His eyes shifted. "But guess who *did* see them?" He winked, but it looked more like a twitch.

"Besides you?"

He shook his head like I was hopeless. "Yeah, besides me." He paused for effect. "Eagleton. He pulled up at the same time as when the lovebirds were saying goodbye. Him and that pretty boy who works for him, Sean something. They rode in one car too." He chortled. "Don't think they spent the night together like Luther and Constance, though."

Sean wasn't important. "How did Eagleton react?"

"Stared at them like he wanted to rip off Luther's manhood. Didn't move until his flunky tugged at him." Ed examined his knuckles. "Just as well. I'd have hated to bust up a fight."

Sure, like a prisoner would hate to beat up a guard. "Anything else?"

He scowled. "Ain't that enough? The guy killed her, sure as hell."

"Maybe. But there's still not enough here to arrest him. My job is to remedy that."

"With my help."

"Of course."

Tucking that bit of information into my memory, I returned to my office in time to pick up a call from my apartment's landlord. He not-so-nicely asked when he could expect my rent check. Thank heaven Gino had the office rent paid up for the entire five-year lease. But that didn't help me with my living arrangements. Talk about a miserable existence. The wood floors in the claustrophobic office creaked like an arthritic man doing deep knee bends and the walls hadn't seen fresh paint since the Clinton administration. The first one. The building didn't have an elevator or a security guard. This place had the charm of a bus terminal.

My chin in my hands, I concluded keeping my living quarters meant working on more than the Adler case. As much as I wanted to solve Constance's murder, it wouldn't provide me with enough money to satisfy my landlord.

Once, one of my cousins scared the pants off me by claiming without money, I'd be forced to roam the streets in torn underwear. Sometimes, late at night, when my sad financial state keeps me awake, I crawl out of bed and ransack my lingerie drawer to make sure none of my underwear is ripped. Afterwards, my adult self reminds me my family would take me in and then I'm able to fall asleep. But that fear, lurks, waiting for me.

I went through my open cases, not that there were many. Advertising could help build the business, but besides having no money for it, the very idea of putting myself on display made my stomach knot up. Lots of people want to be noticed. Not me though. I prefer staying in the background, shrinking away, which makes catching people doing what they shouldn't be doing pretty easy. It doesn't help my income though. If I planned to sleep on something other than the top of my desk, that is.

My tense shoulders ached, but I forced myself to lay all my cases on my desk and found one with the possibility of a quick payoff. Jezebel Jackson wanted to know where her fiancé, Dwayne, went every Tuesday and Thursday night. She'd resorted to hiring me after she'd gotten no satisfactory answers from him. Tomorrow was Thursday. Track him down, and I'd earn the rest of my desperately needed fee.

I stretched and rolled my neck to ease the stress.

Dwayne's photo, the names and addresses of his associates, and all the rest of his information lay in front of me. My camera and I were ready to go.

I took my time getting to my apartment, hoping to miss my landlord. He'd be after me again soon enough. I hated to do it, but asking my father to cover me until Jezebel's final payment seemed like my only option.

Lying in bed that night, I memorized Dwayne's face and that of his friends. Jezebel claimed Dwayne left work about 6:00 in the evening, went back home, then headed who-knows-where. I sort of hoped it wasn't to some other girl. Jezebel was such a sweet woman. Of course, that's no protection against a cheating lover.

That last thought somehow spun me back to Michael. After he popped into my head, concentrating on Dwayne and Jezebel any longer was impossible. Finally, in frustration, I put the photos away and closed my eyes. I dreamed Eagleton chased me with a butcher knife and Corrigan helped him.

The next morning I ran some errands, the last of which was stopping at my dad's. I tried to put it off as long as possible, but knew there was no way asking him for a loan could be avoided. That man's middle name should be Generosity, but I hated to hit him up for money even though it'd only be until Jezebel received my report on Dwayne.

I stepped into my dad's house, feeling like a locust chomping away at all he had. We sat at his kitchen table, and he offered me a hazelnut cherry biscotti and coffee. I automatically said yes, but took just one sip of the hot liquid and merely played with the cookie. It'd be like sawdust in my sand-dry mouth. Staring down at the biscotti like it would do the begging for me, I began. "Dad, I hate to ask, but—"

"You need some money."

I avoided his eyes. "You knew?"

"Figured. How much business you got? Three, maybe four cases? That won't even keep the lights on." His eyes conveyed nothing but concern. "How much do you need?"

I hopped up and threw my arms around his neck. "Enough for this month's rent. I'll pay you back, honest, and by the end of the week."

Dad snorted softly and pulled out his checkbook from his back pocket. He waved his pen at me. "You know, you could always move in with me. Got enough room, that's for sure."

"I love you, Dad, but I've got to make it on my own."

He nodded and it wasn't clear whether he was disappointed or relieved. He wrote out a check for my rent and then some. "Don't worry about paying it back." He handed it to me. "But promise me you'll consider working for your Aunt Lena instead of this, this…" he struggled for the word, "*Che cosa*? This adventure." He covered my hand with his big, calloused one. "Don't keep me worrying about you, Pumpkin."

I plastered on a Mona Lisa smile, hoping he'd never know how much I worried about me too. "I'll think about it. Promise." Merely the thought of working at *Cannoli's* made me want to shriek, imagining myself wiping powdered sugar from the triple chins I'd no doubt acquire. That is, after my aunt married me off to some guy who had more black hair on his back than on his head and a five-o'clock shadow right after he shaved. But I appreciated my father's concern, and adored him for it.

I kissed his cheek and assured him, "I'll be extra careful, Dad."

Leaving my father's house, I drove to the bank and deposited his loan. Then, even blew some bucks on a few groceries. *Ah, the good life!* Once home, I post-dated a check for my rent while shoveling some cereal into my mouth.

By the time I brushed my teeth, my stomach began churning. I didn't relish spying on Wayne any more than reporting my findings to Jezebel, convinced it would break her heart for sure. In that moment of weakness, working at *Cannoli's* didn't sound half-bad.

Michael called and rescued me from any further

despairing thoughts.

"Is something wrong?" *Please, please be okay.*

"I'm fine and cooking veal piccata, but there's too much here for one person. Would you like to come over?"

Visions of delicate veal, drenched in lemon, parsley, and capers waltzed about in my head. My stomach suddenly grumbled at being fed cereal when a feast was so close. But there was Dwayne and Jezebel. I wanted to weep. "It sounds delicious, but I have other business to attend to." My taste buds practically stood up and begged for the veal. Who was I to ignore their basic needs? "On second thought…"

"Yes?" He sounded hopeful.

I released a loud breath. If Gino knew, he would have my license for this. "I have a stakeout tonight. You could come along…"

"And bring the veal?"

I chuckled, happy he caught my drift. "That'd be great. But you should know what you're in for. I spend the evening taking pictures from far away. It's safe, but boring."

He chuckled. "A safe, boring evening sounds great. How soon can you get here?"

We agreed on a time, but on my drive over, guilt over my selfish gluttony replaced my food lust. I didn't know what Dwayne was up to, but it could turn ugly. If Michael got hurt, it'd be my fault. This had to be one of the dumbest things I'd ever done. Michael was a client, a really sweet, adorable one who cooked like a male Julia Child.

I shook my head hard. Gino warned me about letting my heart overrule my head. He didn't say anything about my stomach, though. I fully intended to reverse my rash decision when I got to Michael's home.

Michael was already outside with what looked like a picnic basket when I pulled up. His look of excitement was so cute I couldn't change my mind and disappoint him. Okay, maybe that was just an excuse, but either way, I now had company.

Once we parked close to Dwayne's apartment building, I explained my assignment and recited Gino's advice, "Be close enough to spot him, but far enough so's the pigeon don't notice you."

Michael half smiled and nodded. "Got it."

My stomach felt weighed down, as if each Cheerio I'd eaten earlier had swelled to the size and weight of a marble. Even the scent of glorious veal piccata didn't whet my appetite.

Dwayne finally got into his car and as soon as he pulled away from his apartment, we followed at a discreet distance. Luckily traffic was light and he went the speed limit, making it easy to track him. Michael knew enough to stay silent. I blew out a breath as Dwayne's car pulled up to a row of buildings: one, a convenience store, another, a cleaners, and at the end, a bar that looked like a neighborhood joint where no one knows your name.

I cruised by and observed as Dwayne got out and started toward the bar. Some guy opened the tavern's door, lit a cigarette and watched Dwayne walk past. A lump sat firmly in my throat. This part of the job scared the knickers off of me.

Dwayne continued his trek behind the front building and disappeared. I parked and jumped out of my car, but before I could tell him to stay put, Michael was next to me. We trailed Dwayne and I snapped a photo of him entering a building with red awnings. When he opened the door, lively Latin music blared.

Michael, his eyes wide, whispered, "Do we follow him?"

Staying out of the range of flying fists, just close enough for the camera to get the goods, was my way. But in this case, the blinds were drawn, allowing no way of peering inside. I waited too long to decide, and a stranger approached us from behind. He opened the door and his voice boomed like a carnival barker, "Go on in, folks. We don't bite. I'm Randall Jones, owner of this place." When we didn't move, he smiled. "Cold feet, huh?"

I came out of my haze. "No, no. We were just…walking by."

He let loose with a hearty laugh. "That's what they all say." He hustled us inside and casually blocked the door, making a quick escape difficult. Trapped in the foyer, the music's beat vibrated in my skull. I'd never been this close to the mark, and we only had until the music stopped for good to get any low down on Dwayne.

Before I could throw a plan together, the music abruptly ended. Then, "Well if it ain't Miss $17.95." It was Ed, the lean-and-mean security guard, without his uniform.

Chapter Seven

Ed sidled up to me and chuckled. "Didn't take you for a salsa dancer." He leaned in and his stale-cigarette breath made my nose curl. Spotting my camera, his mouth twisted. "Or are you working a case?" He tilted his chin in Michael's direction. "You're her brother. Constance's, I mean."

The man who'd rushed us in interjected. "Well since you seem to know each other, we're all set." He bustled toward an office in the back.

Michael recovered quicker than me and stuck out his hand to shake Ed's. "Michael Adler. We're just here to dance." Although they shook hands, they reminded me of boxers before their match, each eyeing the other for weaknesses. Ed didn't believe Michael, and Michael didn't trust anyone from Triton.

I spotted Dwayne out of the corner of my eye, standing next to a girl who looked familiar. I didn't want to investigate him now. My frightened psyche sought only to slink back to the car and stuff my face with the veal. I squelched that impulse and addressed Ed, "If you don't mind, we'd like to talk to the instructor."

Ed smirked. "You're looking at him." He bowed low.

My face must have resembled one of those Edvard Munch's portraits of screaming people because Ed followed up with, "Do it part time. With Mallorie." He waved to the overly made-up young woman next to Dwayne. "Hey Mal, come on over."

He whispered to me, "Lose the camera."

This was beyond awful. Next Dwayne would tell me he'd been waiting for me. I slipped the camera into my pocket and hoped no one would notice the bulge. When Mallorie sashayed over, I realized why she looked familiar. She had worked for Constance, her final hire.

Mallorie grinned like we were old friends. "I remember you, you're the private eye."

My eyes darted nervously around the room, wondering if Dwayne had overheard. A suspicious fiancé like Jezebel and a PI that just happens to show up on while he's doing…what? Dancing? I wanted to get out fast, before Dwayne put two and two together and used my camera strap to strangle me. And what would he do to Michael whose only mistake was being a great cook?

Mallorie peered at Michael through her fake eyelashes, talking him up like she wanted him to invest in a Ponzi scheme. Or was that her way of flirting?

I hooked my arm through Michael's. "We better get going. It was nice to see—" But Mallorie slid her arm through Michael's other one and gave it a tug. "No way. You came for a reason."

I gaped at Michael. Before either of us could respond though, Ed piped up, "They came to dance, Mal. Let's show 'em how."

He pulled me away from Michael, signaled to turn the music up, and whirled me around the dance floor. He twirled me out and back in like he was Fred Astaire, but I was Raggedy Ann. When he got me in a clutch he whispered, “She knows more.” With that he spun me out again, smack into Dwayne, who was dancing with a middle-aged woman in spandex pants that probably fit her twenty pounds ago.

I tripped and Dwayne caught me. “Are you okay?”

I righted myself, thankful I hadn’t worn heels. “I’m fine.”

He smiled. “Good. I’m Dwayne. And you’re…?”

“Claire. Just Claire.” I could feel the moisture in my underarms.

“Nice to meet you, Claire.” He motioned toward Michael and Mallorie. “Looks like your friend knows a thing or two about salsa. That’s what I want. Gonna surprise my baby. Her name is Jezebel.”

I felt warm all over, like when a puppy snuggles up to you. “That’s so nice.” I grinned. “So nice.”

Before I babbled further, Ed grabbed hold of me again. “Excuse us, but Claire’s got more to learn tonight.” With that, he whisked me away past Michael. To my amazement and distraction, Michael was gliding around the dance floor like he’d been born to do it.

Through clenched teeth, Ed hissed, “Don’t want you ruining my setup. Mallorie held back with you and the cops. I aim to find out what else she knows.”

“How do you know she’s got anything else?”

Ed held onto my waist while the song ended and another started. “Let’s just say she spends a hell of a lot more than she makes, even with this side job.”

That got my full attention. “So someone’s paying her off.” I panted, slightly out of breath.

He nodded. “But who and why’s the question.”

Missing my spin cue, I mashed his ankle. He winced and dropped his arms. "Ooph!" He rubbed his ankle and murmured, "You're pretty timid as a PI, but you're deadly on the dance floor."

I could feel the others stop and my face felt hot. Michael rushed over, leaving Mallorie to dance solo. "Claire, it's my turn to dance with you." He gave Ed a look that said, "Get lost, pal."

Ed stopped massaging his ankle and stepped back with his hands in the air. "No problemo. But I hope you got steel in your shoes and socks." As he turned to go, he whispered, "Great job. Now I can get back to Miss Mal." He moved in her direction. "Mallorie, may I have this dance?" He only limped a little.

Michael's eyebrows lowered. "Mind if I ask what that was about?"

"Tell you later." A slower musical number started. His hand on my waist felt strong, confident. I relaxed and let him guide me. "Hey, you're pretty good."

He shrugged. "Dancing lessons. My mother insisted my sister and I go." His face clouded over. "Constance made it bearable." He turned his head away and swallowed hard.

The music ended, but we stood still, like a porcelain statue of two dancers, until Mallorie shattered the moment when she clapped her hands. "Break time, everyone."

As the others collapsed into surrounding chairs, I massaged my forehead and sighed, "One of my headaches is coming on." I had to get out of there before my cover got completely blown.

After Michael graciously insisted on paying for our so-called dance lesson, we made our escape to the car, now fragrant with the scent of veal and lemon.

I laid my hand on his arm. "Thank you." In all likelihood, Gino had some rule about not letting a client pay expenses for another client. "I'll pay you back just as soon as this Jezebel pays her balance."

He shrugged. "Forget it. I should thank you. It was fun."

Fun? I was pleased, but sure wouldn't have called it that.

He reached for the casserole and grinned. "Shall we eat?"

"Good idea. We can go to my apar-, ah, office. We'll be more comfortable there."

He thought about it a moment, then said, "We can go back to my place. For dinner."

I wondered if I'd be dessert, picturing myself in just some whipped cream and a cherry, and shivered.

I needn't have wondered. Michael was so engrossed in my recounting of what Ed had told me about Mallorie, I wasn't even an after-dinner mint. My relief mixed with disappointment, neither gaining a foothold.

After my second glass of wine, I slouched in one of his comfy chairs and felt my whole body mellow out. Unfortunately my mouth took the opportunity to sever ties with my brain and I proclaimed, "Michael, you're the best cook around, and a wonderful host, and a charming dinner companion." Thank God, he stopped me before I nominated him for sainthood.

"Thank you, but you make it easy." He blushed.

I blamed it on the wine but I couldn't think of anything witty, so settled for, "Back at ya."

We both fell silent and it seemed like the ticking of his mantle clock got louder. I swirled the wine in my glass and he cleared his throat. *Time for me to say something.* "This was great but I better go." I rose too fast, and the room began to spin. Scared of falling, I latched on to the table, holding as tight as a kid on a roller coaster for the first time. Michael sprang up and grabbed my shoulders for support. Even when the dizziness subsided, he didn't let go. "Are you okay, Claire?"

"Never better." His hands felt good on me and I was afraid if I moved, he'd pull them away. We stood like that for a moment, neither of us going any further.

He must have felt me stiffen just a bit because he dropped his hands and stepped away. "I better clear the dishes."

Offering to help would've been the right thing to do, but sticking around there with him would've been a mistake. I didn't want to get in too deep, at least not until Constance's murder was solved. I stretched and produced a few faked yawns. "Dinner was great, Michael, but it's been a long day. I'll call you when something new turns up."

He walked me to the door where we both stood there like mummies, stiff and brainless. I managed to grab his hand and pumped it. "Thanks again." I practically ran out the door. Not exactly my moment of glory.

***

After a restless night and early morning, my notes on Dwayne's activities lay on my desk in a semblance of order. Jezebel sat in the chair opposite me. Another of Gino's rules was "Don't give them the lowdown 'til they give you the dough."

"As you know, I've completed my investigation."

The woman, in funeral-like garb, sat stiff in her chair,

rubbing her hands together so hard I wondered if they'd spark. Having no desire to prolong her uncertainty, I showed her the photo taken of Dwayne entering the dance studio.

My findings concluded, I smiled, thinking she'd do the same. Or at least show some sign of relief.

Instead, her mouth twisted and her eyes bulged. "You're telling me he wasn't with another woman?"

Didn't she believe me? "No, he isn't. He's just taking dance lessons." I tilted my head. "Isn't that good news?"

She slumped in her chair. "Yeah, it is. But now he'll know I lied."

My eyebrows knit and my stomach tensed. *Why is nothing in this job easy?*

She looked like she was about to cry. "He's taking those damned lessons because I bragged about what a good dancer I was."

My brain screamed, "Stay out of it." But my mouth never took orders from anyone. "What made you do that?"

She leaned her head back like the answer was on the ceiling. "He's great at so many things, I wanted to be better than him at something."

I shrugged. "If it's that important, take lessons yourself."

She shook her head. "Can't afford to. Unless..." A Cheshire cat grin appeared on her face.

I glanced at the check she'd written me like it was a lover who'd just told me we were through. Jezebel's eyes followed mine. "The fee was stated in the contract you signed."

"You're right." She let out a defeated sigh.

I sat back, satisfied, until my sentimental gene began

aggressively reproducing. I gave in and pushed back my practical worries. "Do you know how much they cost?" My voice, barely above a whisper.

Jezebel's eyes sparkled and she looked eighteen, although that birthday was in the distant past. "A friend of mine once offered to teach me off the clock for a hundred dollars."

Subtracting that amount from the total on this case, I pursed my lips. "Can't he be more off the clock than that?" Admitting the stakeout had actually turned out to be pleasant made it easier for me to give in. "Okay, I could subtract $75 from what you owe me right now. You can pay it back at $25 a month." I had a hunch I'd never see that money.

Jezebel pounced. "Really?" She scooped my hand up in hers. "You're great. I mean it. Anytime someone needs an investigator, I'll make sure they have your name."

I rubbed my forehead, already regretting my generosity, especially since it was using borrowed money. Guilt crept up on me. My promise to Dad to repay him with this contract money now became impossible. Not if I wanted to eat and pay Michael back for the dance lessons.

We settled up and an ecstatic Jezebel thanked me even as she walked out my door. She even promised to invite me to the wedding. At least I knew someone who could dance with me there.

Busy berating myself for being a softie, I ignored the phone ringing until I realized the caller was Mallorie. She wanted to meet with me to talk about Constance. That was a shock, and questions boomeranged in my mind, but they went unasked. Afraid of spooking her, I played it cool, keeping my comments to a minimum, and quickly agreeing on a time and place.

Calling Michael crossed my mind. Or maybe Ed. Even Detective Corrigan's name popped into my head, but in the end, I decided it was my case to follow through.

Stuffing two granola bars in my purse, I headed out to meet Mallorie. The congested roads stretched my fifteen minute drive into twenty-five. Frustrated and overheated, I hustled into the café where Mallorie sat at a back table, drinking from a jumbo plastic cup. She tilted her chin towards me, then looked at her cell phone and frowned.

I pulled up a chair. "Sorry for being a little late. Traffic was—"

She nodded. "A bitch, I know, but one of us is on the clock." She scanned the room, then looked straight at me, biting her lower lip.

I thought maybe she needed some prompting. "You wanted to see me about Constance."

Her eyes darted back and forth. "Yeah, I, uh, Ed told me I could trust you."

Good for Ed. "Do you want to talk about who killed Constance?"

She drummed her fingers against her cheek. "Maybe."

I leaned in so close it looked like I was moving in for a kiss. "If you know something, why haven't you gone to the police?"

"Let's just say it isn't in my best interest." She checked the time again. "Can't talk about it now. I gotta get back to work." She glanced around and lowered her voice. "Look, I need help."

One murder, two clients? If this kept up my business would be booming. "Come by at 6:00 tonight." I handed her my card.

She snatched it and without looking at the card or me, she tossed her now empty plastic cup in the trash. Without another word, she hurried out of the café.

Upset with myself about ruining the meeting with Mallorie, I had to make sure my encounter with Ed would be successful so I stopped at the bank. Whatever information he'd provide would require a payment. I withdrew as much as I could afford, and counted each dollar, afraid Ed might withhold a vital piece of information due to a lack of funds.

Ed was leaning against the wall near Triton's back entrance. It was a mystery how the man unearthed anything since he seemed to always be on break. Once he saw me approach, he shook a cigarette out from a crushed soft pack. "Hi there, Miss Private Investigator. What can I do you for?"

"Mallorie contacted me."

He whistled through his teeth. "That was fast. She must be plenty scared."

I had my hand on my wallet, realizing nothing he'd tell me would be free. "What do you know about it?"

He placed his interlaced fingers across his belly. "Depends on the green."

I pulled out a five, hoping that was green enough for him.

He shook his head. "Whatever happened to the twenty we talked about?" He pointed his unlit cigarette at me. "And you still owe me from the last time."

Claiming amnesia might make him angry, so I added a ten to the five. "Here's the rest of what I owe you. How about you advance me your information?"

He threw back his head and laughed. "Have to hand it to you. You've got nerve."

Unfortunately, not much of that, but I kept going. "Once this case is solved, I'll have more than enough money to pay off my debt and then some." My mouth drooped and my sad eyes stared at him as if I was a poor orphan and he was withholding the porridge.

He lit his cigarette, inhaled deeply and blew out a ring of smoke. "I'm already deep in it, so what the hell."

I suppressed a smile, afraid he'd change his mind or think I was taking advantage. Maybe I was a little, but for a good cause. "Thank you." He nodded and I pushed forward. "Are you sure Mallorie is blackmailing someone?"

He looked at me like I'd just asked him if he knew how to spell his name. "And I bet she's squeezin' tight. Not that she admitted as much to me though. My money's on Eagleton for the one she's blackmailing. He probably only took so much, and now he's getting ugly about it."

Nerves started playing a tune in my head and my shoulders stiffened to join in. "So you think she wants me to protect her from the murderer she's blackmailing?"

"You got it." He tilted his chin toward the right. "Don't look now, but Eagleton's flunky is prancing over."

Despite Ed's warning, I turned my head. Sean marched toward us, face puckered like he smelled something rancid. His rant was directed at me. "Why are you back? If it's to harass Mr. Eagleton or anyone else for that matter, I suggest you leave now. We've been more than cooperative."

Ed stepped in. "Whoa, Cowboy. The lady came here to shoot the breeze with me about dance lessons."

A flimsy explanation, but I nodded like some bobble head. "That's right. Ed's a fantastic instructor. Anybody could learn from him, he's..." My words drifted off.

Sean wasn't buying it. "It's plain to see what you're up to." He squinted and crossed his arms. "It's a shame about what happened, but nothing will bring Constance back."

That flippancy got to me. "Finding her killer could bring justice though." I stared right at him, hoping he'd blink first.

Sean averted his eyes and rubbed the back of his neck. "Whatever. You need to leave. This is company property." A vein throbbed in his temple. "No one will talk to you."

"Mallor—" I pressed my lips together, two syllables too late.

Sean's face turned red. "Mallorie? What has she told you?"

"Nothing." I wanted to kick myself. "I just meant—" My mind blanked. "She was friendly."

Ed filled in. "Mallorie's a dance instructor too." He waved his hand in dismissal. "But if Ms. DeNardo shouldn't be here, I'll make sure she stays away."

Sean huffed and gave me the evil eye. "She better." He stomped off.

I glared at Ed. "Thanks for nothing. That shoots my intention of snooping around here."

Ed flicked his cigarette. It arced and landed right in the ashtray/trashcan. "You don't need to. I can do all that while I'm doing my job. No one'll be the wiser."

"Deal. I can use the extra ears and eyes." We shook

hands as I calculated how much all this would cost me.

After leaving Triton I called Michael to let him know about Mallorie coming to my office that evening, but said nothing about my deal with Ed. After the way Michael and Ed had reacted to each other at the dance class, like two rival gang members, it was clear they needed to stay in their own corners. This case was complicated enough without them bumping heads. Plus, I didn't want anything to come between Michael and me. And his veal piccata.

Keeping busy in my office, sorting my numerous bills and trying to figure out which could be paid this month, helped me pass the time. But by 6:00 p.m. everything had been cleared from my desk in anticipation of Mallorie's visit. She'd be the sole focus of my attention.

A quarter after the hour, I wondered if Mallorie had changed her mind, or maybe she wanted to pay me back for my tardiness that afternoon. If either were true, it'd be necessary to revise my plan for getting the lowdown on John Luther, the soon-to-be-president of Triton. He was enamored with Constance and she likely felt equally infatuated with his money and position.

Sean's behavior then popped into my head. He'd seemed awfully, what? Nervous? Irritated? Maybe he deserved another look, especially since he came on so strong during my last visit. He sure didn't want the investigation centering on Triton. But if he was Eagleton's flunky, he could just be following orders from his boss. Still, it might be worthwhile doing some digging on him.

Around 6:20, there was a loud thump against my office door, but I didn't exactly hustle to get to it. If

Mallorie wanted to prove a point by showing up late, she could wait a few seconds. I strolled over and opened the door, ready to greet her with businesslike aplomb. Hard to do though, when her body lay crumpled at my feet. Except for her, the hallway was deserted.

Chapter Eight

I knelt down and pushed back Mallorie's hair to check her pulse. My hands shook so badly it was hard to be sure, but it didn't seem like she had one. I was certain of it upon spotting the thin red line circling her neck.

A cold chill ran down me and I thought I'd be sick. When the worst wave of nausea passed, I pulled myself up, stumbled to the phone and called 911. Rubbing my eyes hard didn't remove the vision of her being murdered right outside my office. The nausea returned full blast when I realized the only thing separating me from the killer had been a plywood door.

The uniformed police came quickly, but not as fast as Detective Corrigan. As if he sat on the edge of his desk chair waiting for me to be involved in something unsavory, like another murder.

While the coroner inspected Mallorie's body, Corrigan scowled at me. "Well, Ms. DeNardo, I see you've been very busy with Triton personnel."

"This wasn't my doing." My voice squeaked like one of the mice in Disney's Cinderella. "Mallorie contacted me. Said she had something to discuss tonight." I pushed my hair from my face with shaky hands.

"Why don't you have a seat," his voice low and comforting. I did just that, preferring not to keel over. He rolled the desk chair around to face me. "Okay, give it to me from the beginning."

For one of the few times in my life, skipping a meal had been a good thing. Second appearances are not pleasant. "She called and said she wanted to talk." I grabbed a tissue and blew my nose. Despite trying to look like I had it under control, my eyes watered and my nose ran. "She wouldn't tell me anything over the phone but she was scared. My advice to her was to go to the police, but she wouldn't listen." Blinking hard to hold back any tears. "She may have been blackmailing Constance Adler's killer."

Corrigan's eyes sparked for a moment, but nothing else betrayed his emotions. In a voice designed to exude calmness he asked, "What makes you think that? Did she give you any hint as to the killer's identity?"

I reached for another tissue. "No." I didn't want to give Ed's part away. "She just said we'd discuss it tonight at our 6:00 appointment." I paused until I could trust my voice. "At 6:20, there was a thump against my door and when I opened it, she was lying there, dead." My fist flew up to my mouth to block a whimper.

For a moment Detective Corrigan watched me try to hold it together. At last he rose and got me a cup of water from the break room. "Maybe she was a blackmailer, maybe not. All we know is, someone wanted her dead. Strangulation marks look like it was done with a thin cord."

He sat down again, our knees almost touching. "Did you see anyone else when you opened the door?"

Shredding the wet tissue, I shook my head. "Didn't hear anything either." My throat tightened. If I had seen or heard anything, my body might have been found next to Mallorie's.

After making sure nobody suspicious was hanging around, the uniformed cops took off, but Corrigan lagged behind. "Will you be okay?"

I nodded, but looked away.

He didn't buy it. "Look, I'm off-duty as of," he glanced at his watch. "an hour ago. Why don't we get out of here and grab some coffee."

Curling up in my bed and hiding under the covers appealed to me more, but I agreed to go. The truth was I didn't need coffee. I needed a pound of chocolate and a stiff drink.

We sat in the coffee shop, him with coffee and me with tea, not saying a word. I rested my chin in my cupped hand to keep it from quivering. Finally Corrigan broke the silence. "It's unfortunate you were the one to find her. First time for a dead body?"

I dropped my hands and absently stirred my tea. "Sorry for not handling it better. PIs are supposed to be made of sterner stuff."

"Maybe, but you're doing okay." He took a sip of his coffee. "Your cases are mostly hubby cheats on wife, or vise versa?"

There wasn't any sarcasm in his voice and he actually looked interested, but now was not the time to give him my autobiography. "I take cases that interest me."

He rubbed his cheek hard. "A little advice. Refund your client's money. This isn't a case for a rookie." After a pause he added, "Another thing. Get a gun and learn how to use it. You'll feel safer and maybe I won't worry as much."

Nothing would have pleased me more than to give up the case and go back to my long distance lens, but Michael depended on me. Corrigan was probably right about getting a gun though.

The detective drained his coffee cup. "It's getting late." He pushed back his chair. "I'll take you to your car and follow you home. Even see you to your door, if that'll make you feel better."

"It would." No use in playing tough. I wanted to stay alive and the night's events scared me so much it was doubtful I'd ever sleep with both eyes closed again. Telling myself Mallorie had been the target, not me, didn't convince the standing-at-attention hairs on the back of my neck to lay down either.

***

I unlocked the door to my apartment and waited in the hallway while Corrigan looked everywhere, in my closets, even under my unmade bed. After a moment, he peeked out the door. "All clear."

"Thank you for going out of your way." My breathing became normal again.

He smiled, showing dimples any female would kill for. "No trouble. I want you to feel safe."

He'd have to sleep on the floor next to my bed, gun drawn, for me to feel safe again. Rather than say that, I said, "It's much appreciated."

His face grew solemn, like lecturing me was next. Instead, he stepped out to stand beside me. "I did find something under the bed. These." He held out a small silky bit of material.

Blood rushed to my face. He'd found my dancing elves Christmas undies. I snatched them from him and murmured something inane like, "Wondered where those were."

Now that he'd checked out my place, I felt foolish and not much of a private investigator. Next I'd be taking Buddy, my stuffed bear, to bed with me.

Buddy's fake fur tickled my nose and woke me up. Just as well since that's when the ringing began. I patted the end table searching for the source of the annoying noise. My phone. No one ever calling that late had good news. My heartbeat sped up a notch. "Hello?"

Silence. Then the caller, sounding like he'd just had throat surgery started to sing a familiar tune. But with very different words.

"First little piggy wanted too much,

Second little piggy knew so much.

Dead little piggy, will you be,

Learning too much, can't you see?"

It felt like someone injected ice into my veins. "Who is this?"

A dial tone was my only answer.

Chapter Nine

I flicked on the lights and scanned my room, knowing in my gut nobody was there. But who hasn't seen all those scary movies where the villain steps out of the darkness? With my mind scattered in terrifying directions, holding myself together seemed next to impossible.

I threw on my clothes and whipped open my apartment door, my can of mace in my hand. *I've got to get a gun.* The hallway was empty. Thank God, since I had no clue what action to take had the killer been there. Pound on old Mrs. Hennessy's door and ask her to call the police?

With the coast clear, I dashed to my car, cranked it up and sped out of the parking lot with no idea where to go. Not to my father's. He worried about me already. While Aunt Lena could kill anyone with her rolling pin, there was no sense in involving her.

My hands ached from gripping the steering wheel, making it even more of a challenge to punch in the number Detective Corrigan gave me. It took two tries to get it right. When he answered, my words tumbled out.

He took a deep breath and exhaled. "Where are you now?"

"In my car, driving…to a friend's house." No sense in giving him details. He might have disapproved.

"Okay, but first thing tomorrow morning, come into the station and we'll see if we can trace the call. We'll also put a tap on your cell and office phones." He paused, and more gently asked, "You'll stay with your friend the rest of the night?"

"Yes."

"Good. And don't put off coming in tomorrow. We need to solve this before anyone else gets hurt." A pause. "Claire?"

"Yes?"

"I'm glad you called me."

My stomach had been lodged in my throat, but it drifted back to its rightful spot. "Me too."

The moment the call ended however, fear took hold again. My foot pressed down hard on the gas pedal, and I sped toward my destination.

Michael's place. Although his lights were on, I struggled with what to say at this hour. Mallorie was dead, and I just received a threat. How's that for the nightly news? I rapped on his front door, feeling foolish and ashamed waiting there in the dark. Gino probably didn't even think he needed to make a rule against a PI running to the client when she was scared. *If he doesn't answer, I'll slip away and he'll never know.*

I was just about to sneak back to my car when Michael, in a tee shirt and sweatpants, opened the door. His jaw dropped like he'd seen a ghost. "Claire. What's wrong? Come inside." He stepped aside and beckoned me in.

It dawned on me; I had arrived at his house unannounced, hair askew, no makeup, most likely a wild look in my eyes. It was the middle of the night and he deserved an explanation. My face burned and my words tumbled out. "I shouldn't be bothering you. It's just this threatening call…"

Michael's eyes opened bigger than pasta plates. He placed a protective arm around my tense shoulders. Its warmth began to thaw my scared stiff body. "Sit down."

He planted himself across from me. "Are you all right? What did the caller say?"

I looked down at my hands. "He pretty much told me to butt out of Constance's murder case or be the next one…" I choked on the last word, "dead." After a moment added. "Mallorie was murdered tonight. Strangled right outside my office door."

He bent over in his chair and wrapped my hands in his large ones. "I've had a bad feeling all night. Do you want to call the police?"

"Already did. They think if there's another call they could trace it." I didn't tell him Corrigan also advised me to back off the case.

"No more calls. I'll pay you the balance if you'll drop this case. It's not right you risking your life."

Biting my tongue stopped me from screaming, "Okay!" It was now impossible to drop this case. First, my sense of right versus wrong wouldn't let me. "I can't."

His look of disbelief mixed with annoyance made me realize Michael needed a more sensible explanation than my just channeling John Wayne. "What if the caller doesn't realize I've dropped the investigation and kills me anyway?"

He rose and began to pace. "Claire, you shouldn't go on with this. It's too dangerous." He halted and squatted next to me, clasping my upper arms tightly. "We could find a way to let the killer know. Please."

"How? Rent out a billboard saying I'm off the case?"

Despite my sarcastic response, the idea took root in my mind. That is, until my conscience butted in. If the killer went on to murder someone else, my guilt would be unbearable. "Can't give up yet, Michael. It won't be as dangerous if I work closer with the police. They'll keep me safer." *Sure, about as safe as confronting an angry grizzly with a water gun.*

He turned away, hiding his reaction, but when he faced me again, he blew out a breath. "We don't have to discuss it this minute, because…" A mischievous smile appeared. "Couldn't sleep so I made chocolate apricot oatmeal cookies. Let's have some. Then we can talk."

I'm usually of the belief cookies cure anything, but doubted even they would make me feel better. Maybe the apricots might even catch in my constricted throat. Michael insisted the cookies, eaten slowly, were safe.

He thoughtfully handed me a glass of wine instead of the expected coffee or milk. "Here, drink this. I do believe white goes well with cookies." He placed a plate of the baked goodies near me and sat down. "You should spend the night here." He grabbed a cookie. "I mean, in the guest room." He looked down at his hands and I could swear he blushed. "Unless you'd rather…"

While it was tempting to find out where 'rather' might lead, I had enough to deal with. "The guest room would be fine." My glass stood empty. It was 2:00 in the morning and my eyelids drooped. The wine had done its job.

Michael yawned, "Want a refill?"

I shook my head, stood up and stretched. "I've kept

you awake too long. How about we both get some sleep?"

He showed me to the guest room and handed me an extra blanket, a travel toothbrush and toothpaste. The man was definitely prepared for guests.

"Appreciate it, Michael."

He waved away my thanks. "It's my fault you're in danger. I'm the one who's sorry."

I placed my hand flat on his chest and could feel his heartbeat. "I'm not." *Why couldn't we have met at a party, or been introduced by a friend?*

His heart sped up a bit more and he smiled. "You don't have to stay in the guest room."

We embraced. Despite my being so petite, and him 6', we fit well together. Before our bodies got too comfortable though I stepped back, wished him a goodnight, and closed the door behind me, knowing that was the smart thing to do. He was my client and for now, that was all he could be.

Fear and panic from this evening sapped everything out of me. Without some rest my foggy brain would be useless. Plus, the faster this case got wrapped up, the sooner I could act on my baser instincts.

My last waking thought was about going to the police station and then back to my office for Ed's phone number.

I woke up after a short, restless sleep and realized it was 4:30 in the morning. There was one new message on my phone. My stomach felt like it had shriveled to the size of a prune and the wine tasted sour in my mouth. I grabbed the towel and toothbrush and headed to the bathroom, willing myself not to check my messages yet. But curiosity overcame my sense. I should have listened to my sense.

"This is Detective Corrigan. It's really late, or early, depending on your point of view. Anyway, I'll be in touch."

What was that about? His voice was almost friendly, except for the part about being in touch, which could've been a threat.

After dressing, I opened the bedroom door and tiptoed out. Since Michael didn't appear to be up yet, I scribbled a note to thank him and promised to call him later in the day.

My eyes struggled to stay open on the way to my office. Once I arrived, I collapsed onto the loveseat. Not the most comfortable piece of furniture, but with exhaustion such as this, even a bed of nails would have suited me.

About flipping around for the past forty minutes or so, I finally resigned myself to starting the day.

First order of business was a cup of tea, with the hope that the caffeine would boost my energy level. Then on to my notes on Constance's murder. Eagleton still got my vote, but his wife, or John Luther, Constance's final lover, merited closer looks. I wondered if it was too early to call Ed. What did he do at night anyway? Shoot pool? Attend cock fights? No time for humor with Constance's murderer still loose. For Michael's sake and my own safety, finding the killer superseded everything else.

On the last sip of tea, my promise to visit Detective Corrigan came back to me. I added that to my list of need-to-do's. But it wasn't at the top.

My office phone rang, startling me. "Hello?"

"Claire? Ed here. Meet me at the Owl Diner. It's one street over from Triton, on Detroit. Got some juicy stuff you need to hear."

I pulled an errant hair out of my mouth. "How did you know to call the office?"

"Lucky guess." He paused, and I could picture him with a smirk on his face. "How about it? Say in an hour?"

My stomach growled, reminding me my last meal had been one cookie. I didn't feel hungry but Ed's information might whet my appetite. "See you there."

So much traffic on a Saturday. It took me a while to get there, plus I didn't see the place and drove by it twice. Turned out, the Owl was a hole-in-the-wall greasy spoon with ripped pleather booths and waitresses who called you Hon. I hurried in; Ed had already dug into a plate of enormous pancakes.

He waved his loaded fork at me. "About time you got here. Want some cakes?" He called to the waitress.

His butter and syrup-laden pancakes looked delicious, but I wasn't up to that. "A cinnamon bagel. No butter or cream cheese."

He grimaced. "Jeez, no wonder you got no meat on your bones."

Obviously, the man was delusional. "What've you got for me?"

He shoveled in a bite and with his mouth full, mumbled, "Mallorie's dead."

"Tell me something I don't know." I raised an eyebrow. "But how did you find out?"

He pushed away his plate and burped into his hand. "Cops came around, snooping. Must have been about 6:30 or 6:45 last night. Anyway, they questioned everyone still at Triton. They also wanted to know who wasn't at work and should've been."

"And?" He had to have more information than that.

"And..." He stuck his tongue between his teeth and sucked. "Eagleton left early yesterday. So did his go-for, Sean."

My spine straightened. "Do the police know?"

He looked at me like I'd asked him what a bear does in the woods. "You kiddin' me? Course they do. I told 'em."

"But you don't like cops."

"Someone had to tell them. Might as well have been me. Lots of people noticed them gone. Maybe now the cops will really put the screws on and Eagleton will slip, you know?" He leaned back a little and squinted at me. "You're not lookin' so healthy. Like real pale." He glanced around the restaurant. "Hey, how'd you know about Mallorie so soon?"

I gave him the rundown of the previous night's events, including that frightening call. But, not wanting him to think I crossed to the other side, left out calling Corrigan. My description must have whetted his appetite because he drew his plate back, slowly pouring more syrup on what was left of his breakfast. If he didn't say anything soon, I'd fall asleep, with my bagel as a pillow.

He recapped the syrup bottle. "So that's why you look like hell."

"Thanks for the compliment." I leaned forward and hissed, "I happen to be trembling in my suede boots." There was more to my feelings than that. Slowly, my anger revealed itself and I slapped my palm against the Formica table. "You know, whoever killed Constance and Mallorie wants me out of the picture. So I'm staying in."

Ed ran his tongue over his lower teeth and smiled.

"Atta girl."

The waitress sauntered over, "You two finished?" We nodded and she dropped off the bill. I reached out, but Ed grabbed it. "After the night you had, the least I can do is buy you a bagel."

When we stepped outside, he lit a cigarette and inhaled deeply. "It's time we rattled Sean's cage. I'm guessing he ain't got it in him to kill someone, but he knows something."

"Maybe so, but shouldn't we wait to see what the police turn up?" I regretted the question as soon as it came out. It made me sound timid, hesitant, not a good thing. For us to work together well, Ed had to stop thinking of me as a little lost girl, so I added, "But it'd be better if we figured it out on our own."

Ed nodded his approval. "Got that right." He pulled a thick metal ring full of various keys and dangled them in front of me. "Bet we could learn a lot about Sean and Eagleton just by seeing what they have in their offices."

The gleam in his eyes worried me. He actually enjoyed this, while my head pounded as soon as he jangled that mess of keys. "What if someone sees us?" My voice went so high, I'm surprised dogs didn't come running. "Plus, Triton is off limits to me, remember?"

Ed looked sideways at me. "First, it's Saturday. You actually think management works Saturday mornings? Besides, it's no biggie to turn off the security cameras." He shook the keys once more. "Come on. We'll be in and out. We'll take my car in case anyone does come in. We don't want that extra trouble."

I began to sweat and wished for some deodorant. "All right. Let's make it quick."

I fidgeted all the way over while Ed sang along to his

old timey country music. By the time he screeched his last yodel, my head threatened to break into two pieces.

We made it into the research and development department without incident. I took Sean's smaller office and Ed headed to Eagleton's. My headache finally settled down to a hard pound, but my mouth was dry enough to plant cactus. I worked fast, considering how bad my hands shook. Good Catholic girls didn't ransack offices that weren't theirs. If we found something, would stealing it still be a sin?

In spite of risking a nervous breakdown, my search proved fruitless. Before I could let Ed know, a woman's righteous voice rang out.

"Ed Horwath. What are you doing in Mr. Eagleton's office?"

That bagel threatened to make a return appearance as I ducked behind Sean's bookcase and tried to make myself as small as possible. Bad enough Ed got caught. She'd call the police on me for sure.

His voice boomed. "Good morning to ya, Tara. I was just checking to make sure the cops didn't mess up Mr. Eagleton's office too much last night."

Tara's tone indicated she didn't believe him. "You shouldn't be in there without Mr. Eagleton."

Ed purred, "Well you might be right about that. Only just got here when you saw me, but I'll be on my way. You have a good day, Tara." He whistled as he walked away.

Oh, good God, Ed. Don't you dare leave me here. I shivered, picturing myself arrested and strip searched. My wrists could almost feel the cold, steel handcuffs around them.

Chapter Ten

It seemed like an hour passed, but it was probably more like ten minutes. My bladder, though, didn't know the difference. I cursed the tea at the restaurant, and shifted from foot to foot. When that didn't work I imagined being surrounded by an arid desert. Useless. If something didn't happen soon, there could be a puddle on Sean's carpet.

From the sound of it, Tara was now at her desk in the outside office, closing drawers and hitting computer keys. A full bladder was bad enough, but then my left leg fell asleep. I tried to move it and tipped over, knocking my head against a massive Physician's Desk Reference manual. It tumbled off the shelf but I caught it, bending my fingers way back and ripping fingernails. A business card slid out from the middle of the tome. "Biologic Solutions, Inc., George Workosky, RPh, V.P. Research & Development."

The guy's phone number and email address followed. On the back someone, probably Sean, had written, "Cafe Palermo, 6:00 Friday night." Meaning, Sean and Eagleton must have been there last night. Being without a pen, my only option was to memorize the outsider's contact information.

With my eyes closed, trying to imprint the numbers on my brain, I didn't hear the approaching footsteps. But the loud intake of startled breath did get through to me.

"What are you doing here?" Tara stood there, feet apart, clutching a letter opener.

Jumping up so fast caused me to totter, and I grabbed onto the bookshelf to steady myself. The overloaded piece of furniture toppled over, diverting Tara's attention long enough for me to come up with the most absurd excuse ever. "Sean told me to come by and pick up a book he told me about." I inwardly cursed my lack of imagination.

She scowled. "You expect me to believe that?" She puckered her lips and her eyebrows lowered. "Wait a minute. You're that private detective who came snooping around after Constance died."

I forced myself to smile like a politician and stuck out my hand. "You're right. Glad to see you again, Tara."

She ignored my hand. "Did Ed let you in? He should be fired. I'd call security on you, but today, that's Ed. Maybe I should call the cops on both of you."

Oh, crap on a crepe. I held up my hand. "No! Wait. First hear me out. It wasn't Ed's fault. I, I practically threatened him with my mace." I pulled out the tiny can to demonstrate. "Maybe nobody told you, but Mallorie was murdered on my doorstep. Do you have any idea how scary and upsetting that is? Sleeping is impossible. If I don't figure this out soon, it'll make me crazy." I held my breath. If she didn't accept this, next up was my natural defense, sobbing and begging.

At least now it didn't look like she planned to stab me with her letter opener. "But why are you looking in Sean's office? You can't possibly think he's involved in murder. That man is practically a saint with what he puts up with. And he never complains." She glanced toward his desk. "Although…"

I tried to sound casual. "Although?"

She waved her hand as if batting an annoying fly. "Nothing. Just that Sean did look awfully nervous yesterday. We had a meeting late in the afternoon, and he couldn't keep his mind on it. Kept looking at the clock and checking his phone messages."

She stopped abruptly and went back to looking at me as if deciding whether or not to have me guillotined. "Never mind. Okay. It may not be the smartest thing to do, but I'm letting you go. Mallorie wasn't my favorite person. Still, whoever killed her should be caught." Her eyes narrowed. "Don't come back."

"Never again. Ever. Thank you so much." I stepped out of Sean's office. "Just one thing." I bit my lower lip. "Mind if I use the bathroom?"

She huffed, but led me to the closest one and followed me in like a high school monitor. I made up a rule Gino probably didn't think of. Never drink tea before snooping.

Tara made sure Triton's outside door would lock behind me. When it did, Ed came out of the shadows.

My upper lip curled. "Thanks for nothing. She was going to turn me over to the police."

He waved off my concern. "I was coming back for you. Didn't count on you giving yourself away so soon. I wanted to wait until Tara went to the break room for coffee." He chuckled, "She steals a pack of it about once a week. Thinks no one notices." He continued, "Anyway, I didn't find zilch. But then, Tara interrupted me."

I told him about finding the business card. "According to Tara, Sean was antsy yesterday afternoon. Maybe because of that 6:00 meeting with this guy, Workosky."

Ed scratched his head. "Could be. Let's go check it out."

"No need for you to come, Ed." It was great having his help, but it wasn't fair to him. Besides getting into trouble with the police, he could lose his job over this. He could also be in as much danger as me. And, to tell the truth, I wasn't even sure there'd be any money to pay him.

Ed wasn't about to be deterred. "No way, Jose. This is getting good. Hell, I'm not even counting on the money you owe me. I'm in. No argument."

My wholehearted trust in Ed was still forming, but there was little doubt in my mind his muscle could come in handy. Of course, I'd probably need to take a second job at Aunt Lena's to pay him. That assumed we both survived this case.

We drove back to the Owl to get my car. "My theory is Eagleton and Sean are jumping ship and met with this Workosky guy last night. If that's the case, though, neither of them could be Mallorie's killer."

Ed drummed his steering wheel and thought out loud. "That would explain them leaving early, but one of them could've slipped out long enough to do the job and come back. He could have said he was in the john with belly problems."

I grimaced. "You don't do that if you're trying to impress someone."

He shrugged. "A guy might."

We passed a billboard advertising bathroom renovations. That ad, plus the noticeable failure of my deodorant, overwhelmed me with the desire for a hot shower. When Ed pulled up next to my car, I opened the door and said, "Give me an hour. After that, I'll be ready for anything."

He shot me a cocky smile. "Sure thing. But instead of cooling my heels, waiting, think I'll try my luck with Luther's office."

Parked in my assigned spot in my apartment's lot, I didn't leave the car until sure nobody was stalking me. My heart raced, urging me toward the building's door and up the stairs to my place. *Please, please don't let someone be inside.*

A can of mace in my hand, I threw open the door and scanned the room while listening for any out-of-the-ordinary noise. Nothing. With both feet inside, I spun like cops do on television. Convinced the place was clear, I locked my door behind me and blew out a relieved breath, but sucked it back in when my phone rang. *Thank God for caller ID.*

"Where have you been?" It was a very irate Aunt Lena. "This is the third time I've called."

I checked my phone. Three missed calls. *Was one from Corrigan?* "Do you need something?"

My aunt's voice was honey on a buttermilk biscuit. "I know it's short notice, but can you fill in for your father again tonight? Just a few hours. And bring that nice boy, Michael, with you."

My shoulders slumped and I wanted to revolt like the surliest teen. Instead, "What time do you need me?"

It wasn't hard to picture her crafty grin. "From 7:00

to 9:00. And you'll bring Michael?"

Biting my lip hard stopped me from scolding her for attempted matchmaking. "I don't know if he'll come."

"You'll ask him, though." Not a question, not even a request.

I turned my face to heaven and begged for patience. She meant well. "Yeah, but he may have other plans."

"He may not. Ask him."

After I practically cut her off, I stomped into the bathroom and came out again to make sure my door's deadbolt was on. My phone lay on the sofa, within easy reach and beckoning to me. Despite being irritated when my aunt brought it up, having Michael come along on Saturday seemed like a wonderful idea. I could claim my aunt wanted to see him again. After all, she did.

Michael didn't answer his phone, so after leaving a message, I returned to the bathroom and hoped to feel better after my shower. My skin tingled from the beads of hot water that fell. The rhythm of the water calmed me enough so that, for a brief moment, I believed everything would turn out fine.

Combing my hair, I stared into the mirror, not seeing, concentrating on what to say to Michael when we talked next. When I did notice my reflection, that woman had a soft smile on her face.

Too bad my phone went off and interrupted the pleasant interlude. Wrapping the towel around my still damp body I rushed to answer it. Probably Aunt Lena to find out Michael's answer.

It was Detective Corrigan. "Hi Claire. Called you again last night to make sure you were okay. I was concerned."

I kept my explanation short and dishonest. "Thank

you for that. Everything is fine. My friend and I couldn't sleep, so we went for coffee." A clump of hair fell into my eyes. In my attempt to push it back, my towel fell off. I bent down to pick it up and banged my head on the table. "Ooph." I rubbed the now sore spot and dropped the towel again, but let it lay.

"You okay?"

"Just hit my head." Rather than explain about being naked, I changed the subject, moving into the personal stuff. "When you called, I thought you were my aunt. She's playing Cupid." *Why did that come out of my mouth?* It wasn't his business.

His laugh sounded warm and genuine. "I get it. My family does the same thing. Being single can be tricky. Everyone wants you to find someone." For a second there was an awkward silence. He cleared his throat. "I also called you earlier to ask if you remembered anything else from last night." His tone switched and we were back to business. "Like agreeing to come into the station first thing?"

My hand flew up to my mouth. "On my way there." It had unbelievably slipped my mind.

"You better be." He paused. "Whether you realize it or not, I'm concerned about you. Don't want to see your body. I mean, shot, or strangled. You know, dead."

His sudden verbal awkwardness struck me as sweet, but before I could respond, he hung up.

All the way to the police station my mind fought against remembering the details of last night's phone call. Distracted, I ran a red light and laid on my horn, hoping no cars had driven into my path. Thank God for clear intersections. My memories of last night could wait until reaching my destination.

When I pulled up to the station, Detective Corrigan was waiting. He greeted me with a wry smiled. "So you finally made it."

"Nice to see you, too."

We wound our way back to his desk, and after an attempt at getting me to relax, Corrigan asked me to repeat the ugly words the killer had spoken. They flashed through my mind as if they'd been spoken that same moment. My palms moistened as I painstakingly recited them. I blinked to keep the tears from rolling down my cheeks.

He leaned in, elbows on his thighs. "Claire, let's see if we can figure out whose number that was." He took my phone and called a woman over. "This is Julie Chou. She's going to see what she can find out about your caller."

He said a few words to the woman then turned back to me. "Did you detect any accent or unusual speech pattern?"

"No."

"Any background noises, like a horn or train or anything?"

"No, but..."

"But what?"

"He sang his message."

Corrigan cocked his head. "Sang it? Do you remember the tune?"

My face scrunched up in an effort to recall. Usually, I get earworms, that annoying repetition of a song. It doesn't matter what era it's from or whether it's a favorite song or not, it just plays over and over in my head. But the caller's tune wasn't one of those. "No idea, but it sounded familiar like, you know, 'Jingle Bells'."

"He sang Christmas carols?"

"No! But it was a tune I've heard before. Maybe it was a theme song from a show he liked."

"Hmmm. Well, keep trying to remember it. Could be important." He asked me more questions I couldn't answer and, by the time he was done, we were both frustrated.

He rotated his neck and it made cracking noises. "At least if you get another one, you know what to pay attention to. And with the phone tap we'll be able to listen in."

My shoulders tightened. "You don't think he'll call again."

He looked me in the eye. "Unfortunately he will." He leaned in toward me. "Claire, drop this case. You're in over your head."

In other words, I should light some candles, and pray to not get murdered. But letting go of this case wasn't an option. "Appreciate your concern."

He continued to stare at me, then sat back in his chair and chewed on his lower lip. "Not gonna do it, are you?"

I didn't want him angry, knowing he might be the only one between me and the phone-calling killer. "You're right, of course, but…"

He closed down the case file and rested his hands flat on his desk, as close to me as he could be without touching me. "If you stay on this case, you could end up on the list of victims."

No words could describe my mixed-up feelings, so rather than try to explain, I looked away.

"Unbelievable." He walked off to retrieve my phone and handed it to me. "If we get anything on that number, I'll let you know."

"Thank you." I stood and offered him my hand. He shook it firmly and, it seemed to me, held it a second longer than necessary.

Outside the safety of the police station, working at *Cannoli's* started looking better and better. Inhaling deeply, I put that idea to rest. There was a case to solve.

Back at my office, I googled Biologic Solutions to see if any relationship with Triton existed. Seems they weren't competitors, since each had products to service a different segment of the medication-taking population. I switched my search to George Workosky and found out he was the new boy wonder of Biologic Solutions, linked with research in holding back the aging process. So far there were no new drugs in the pipeline, but according to one press release, production of anti-aging pills sat just over the horizon. Triton's press releases didn't mention any similar research.

Two hours later and I was still no wiser about why Sean and Eagleton had met with Workosky. One bit of information helped. Biologic Solutions was headquartered in Connecticut, so maybe Workosky flew in to meet with Sean and Eagleton. Cafe Palermo, the restaurant where they probably met, was located in the Majestic Hotel. Workosky might be staying there.

I paced back and forth, debating the wisdom of visiting him. My common sense urged me to do so. My imagination, sometimes the ruling party of my brain, ran wild. *What if he was the killer?* I took a deep breath to calm myself. Then called Ed.

Ed's assurance was tinged with impatience. "Workosky's a pharmacist, not a gangster."

I scowled and defended my skittishness. "But maybe he has a sideline, like a hired assassin."

He sighed. "Yeah. Maybe if Constance and Mallorie had been poisoned. Otherwise, it's not likely he killed them."

Even though Ed didn't believe Workosky had anything to do with the murders, it was a relief when he agreed to meet me at the Majestic and be my backup, if needed.

We entered the Majestic's lobby and overheard the clerk at the registration desk address a fair-haired, early forties-looking man. "Was everything to your liking, Mr. Workosky?"

Ed pointed at Workosky and mimed what my actions should be. To which I vehemently shook my head.

Watching our quarry turn to leave, though, I was forced to say something. "You're George Workosky?" As soon as he nodded, my tongue tied itself up and, to my horror, no more words came out. Luckily, I stood between him and his suitcase, and when he hesitated to move around me, I whipped out one of my business cards and handed it to him. I winced at the smear of chocolate on it and in that second, my ability to speak returned."I'm Claire DeNardo, Private Investigator, working on the murder of—"

He held up his hand. "Already talked to the police. Look, I have a plane to catch, so if you'll excuse me..." He reached around to grab his bag. I stepped sideways, ready to let him get away. Only Ed's bugged-eyed look stopped me.

"Just a couple questions." He wasn't stopping and I panicked. "How would you like a ride to the airport?" My stomach sunk, realizing a potential murderer would be riding in my car. Just the two of us.

Out of the corner of my eye I could see Ed look down

and rub his forehead. It was obvious he thought my actions bordered on lunacy.

Workosky squinted at me and a smile curled the corners of his mouth. "Why not? I don't often have a pretty woman chauffer me around."

I imagined turning as pale as Workosky's hotel receipt. "Great."

He bowed and with a sweeping gesture said, "Lead the way."

If only Ed would come to my rescue. But my mouth, acting independently from my brain, got me into this. It had to get me out.

Workosky made a sweeping gesture. "You lead, I'll follow."

A part of me hoped my cantankerous old car wouldn't start.

The pharmacist laid his suitcase in my car's trunk and climbed in the front passenger's seat. To my relief, Ed texted me he'd tail us. A couple deep breaths to steady myself. "Fasten your seatbelt, please." If he planned on murdering me, it might take him longer strapped in.

As soon as we got on the road and Ed pulled his car behind me, I began to grill Workosky. "You were in town just to meet with Brody Eagleton and Sean Lawrence?"

"Now what makes you think that?"

Relieved not to be facing him, I boldfaced lied. "Police informed me." My hands begged to be released from my death grip on the steering wheel. "And how long did your dinner meeting last?"

"The police didn't tell you?"

I was driving the car, but getting nowhere. "Would you mind telling me what you talked about?"

He shrugged. "Small talk, you know."

Why is this so much easier on TV? "For two hours? What was the purpose of the meeting? You could at least tell me that."

He chuckled. "You could've saved yourself a trip to the airport. I don't know. The guest of honor didn't show up, so dinner turned out purely social. End of story."

He looked at me like a dog would at a new rawhide chew. "Had we met earlier, we could have had dinner together instead. It would've been much more…pleasurable."

When Hell freezes over and Satan makes popsicles. Why was I irresistible to rodents like this guy? I quickly exempted Michael from that long-tailed group. It took a lot of self-control to ignore Workosky's contemptible come-on, but there was no other choice if I wanted information. "Who was this fourth person?"

He waved my question away. "Let's not talk about that. Tell me about yourself. Are you involved with someone?" The look on his face made me want to put more clothes on. "Actually, it'd be even better if you were. Forbidden fruit and all." He leaned in toward me as much as the seatbelt allowed and leered, "I'll be back in town soon. I could extend my visit another day—or night." His eyebrow arched. "Get you a key to my hotel room."

This guy wasn't a killer. He was a sleaze bucket. I stuck out my arm to keep him at a distance. "Let's get back to last night."

"Why talk about last night when there can be future nights for us to think about?"

"There is no *us*. Never will be."

He held up his index finger to make a point. "Never

say never."

"What was the topic supposed to be?"

He looked out the passenger door window. "Mr. Eagleton told me he had a proposition for me. That's all I know."

My eyes narrowed. "You came all the way out here without knowing why?"

He tilted his head to his right. "There's my terminal."

I pulled up to the passenger unloading area. Keeping the car locked until he answered my question did occur to me, but in all likelihood there'd only be more disgusting leers. At least I knew another person was involved in last night's meeting.

Once Workosky enter the airport ticketing area, I blew out a big breath and waved to Ed, who pulled up beside me. He got out of the car and leaned his head through my open window. "Everything okay, kiddo? What's the lowdown?"

"Only that someone else was supposed to join them. It could be a he or a she."

He rubbed his chin. "Mallorie, maybe?"

"Who knows?" I sighed loudly. "Let's go back to the restaurant and see if Workosky told the truth about the time of day."

Workosky's sudden reappearance and his banging on the passenger side window jarred me. "Forgot my bag." He grabbed his suitcase from my popped trunk and gave Ed the once-over. His upper lip curled and he spat, "She turned me down for *you*?" He sprinted back into the terminal without even a look back.

Ed snorted. "Pleasant chap."

"I've met some who were worse. But not many." Changing the subject, I said, "I'm going over to Cafe

Palermo to see if Workosky's story checks out. If it does, that could explain why Sean was as jumpy as Tara said. He was waiting for the third person to call and confirm."

"Could be. After we finish with the restaurant, I'm heading to Luther's office to have a look-see. Maybe spin around in the big boss's chair."

The trip to the restaurant was a waste. The three men, Eagleton, Workosky, and Lawrence, must not have made much of an impression at dinner. The waiter had a vague memory of the men and the bartender recalled the drink Sean ordered, an exotic mix the bartender had to look up.

After that, Ed and I split up, him to Luther's office, and me, my apartment. Thinking about that awful phone call made me dread going home, but I needed some downtime before putting in the hours at *Cannoli's*.

Speaking of which, I checked my messages. Michael had called, saying he'd be happy to accept my, or rather my aunt's invitation. Mixed feelings of delight and uneasiness surprised me.

Thinking about *Cannoli's* reminded me of my father, whom I hadn't seen for a few days. No matter what, Dad was always the one I counted on. Try as I might, my daughtering skills weren't always up to par, though.

Aunt Lena never said why Dad wouldn't be helping tonight. A good daughter would have asked why, even knowing he probably just had other plans. If something was wrong with him, I assured myself Aunt Lena would be the first to know and tell me. Still, time for a father-daughter visit.

In response to my knock on his door, Dad yelled, "Come on in. It's open." I sighed, knowing it was time to remind him again about keeping his door locked, even when he was home. Sure, it was still the old neighborhood, but even old neighborhoods weren't truly safe anymore.

He rose from his recliner and turned down the television. It was some documentary on artificial insemination of elephants. My dad obviously wasn't picky about what he watched. We hugged our hellos. "Dad, you need to lock your door."

"I know, I know. Just sometimes I forget." He smiled. "Hey. Want some meatballs? Lena brought them over. She's afraid I'm gonna starve." He patted his belly. "No chance of that."

Nothing says love better than my aunt's meatballs and my dad sharing them with me. "Of course. You're going to have some too, aren't you?"

"Sure. A little pasta with it?" He headed into the kitchen with me following.

"Just a couple meatballs. A girl has to watch her figure."

His kitchen wall phone rang, and without thinking, I answered.

At first no one spoke. Figuring it was a telemarketer who had delayed hanging up, I was ready to hang up when a raspy, chilling voice began to sing. The tune was different than the last time, but the voice, just as familiar.

"Little piggy.
Told you before, you're a piggy.
Sticking your pig snout
Where it does not belong, you see.
Little piggy
Say it loud you'll be dropping the case
Say it not and your life I'll erase.
Little piggy."

Chapter Eleven

My hand flew to my mouth and I dropped the phone like it was a hot coal. How had the killer gotten my father's phone number? How did he know who'd answer the call? My mind spun, at once telling me not to react, not to scare my father. The next second, nothing would do but to curl up on his lap and hide from the world.

My father spun around. He dropped the wooden spoon he'd been using and rushed over to me. "What's wrong? Claire, who was it?"

Although autumn was hanging on keeping it somewhat warm, it felt like an icy wind had blown over me and I shivered.

He took me into his arms and gave me a Daddy hug, the kind of embrace meant to protect me from every imagined monster. If only it could do the same with this very real one. After a moment he released me. "What did they say to you?"

My eyes couldn't meet his dark, worried ones. "Just a very nasty obscene call. One of those random things."

"Oh, Pumpkin. I should've answered."

"It's okay, Dad." I inhaled deeply and stepped over to

the window above the sink, peering out, hoping the killer wasn't lurking about. My stomach felt like someone had tied it up like you would a pork roast.

"What are you looking for?"

"Uh, just wanted to see if it was raining." There wasn't a cloud anywhere. "Dad, my appetite is gone. Do you mind if I skip the meatballs?"

He raised one bushy black-mixed-with-grey eyebrow. "That must've been one hell of an obscene call. Something else is going on. Is it one of your cases?" Reaching for me, he continued, "Please, for my sake, just tell whoever hired you on this latest case that you can't stay with it. I lost your mother. It'd kill me if anything happened to you."

Tears rimmed my eyes, but I refused to let them fall. It'd be the same for me if I lost him. Terror, along with tremendous guilt, took turns inside me. Hatred for this killer burned through me. It'd break my heart if my father came to any harm, either physically or emotionally.

It now hit home how vulnerable my father was. The man couldn't even remember to lock his door. He needed protection, without knowing he had it. Corrigan flashed in my mind.

My task right now was making Dad believe everything would be all right. "I'll talk to the client."

"If it's about money, I'll give you whatever you need. It's not worth it, Pumpkin."

I hung my head, embarrassed, like when Dad caught me kissing Jimmy Sarrotti, the kid who had lived next door.

He hugged me again. "I told you before, you could move back in with me."

The thought of my dad waiting up each time I was out late, checking out my dates horrified me. What if he wanted me to talk about my cases? "Your offer is really appreciated, Dad, but…"

"But you'd rather not live here again." He put his hand up to stop my protests. "I get it. But know you're always welcome."

I kissed his cheek, realizing for the millionth time what a great guy my father was. He deserved whatever it took to protect him. A moment passed before I could seize an opportunity. "Forgot something in the car. Be right back."

Sitting inside my car, arms pressed hard against my stomach, the tears impossible to shed in front of my father flowed. As soon as my hands stopped trembling enough to punch in his number, I called Corrigan. He picked up on the first ring.

"What's up, Claire? You okay?"

"He called me at my father's house."

"Dammit. Is your father okay? Should I send someone over?"

I blew out a long breath. "He doesn't know about the first call or that this second one threatened me again. Still, can you have someone in an unmarked car watch over him? No black-and-whites. That'd just scare him."

The sound of shuffling papers. "Okay, I'll get one over there ASAP. Let me have his address and phone number. We'll trace the call too."

My shoulders dropped and the tension dissipated. I gave him the information he needed and thanked him.

"No thanks needed. Now your father's involved, though. It's time to back out of the case."

But it wasn't. Now that the killer had my father's

phone number and probably his address, the dirt bag might go after him to get to me. I bit my lower lip hard. Fear for my father burrowed in my gut like a worm in fresh dirt.

"We'll see."

"Claire, you can't—"

I pressed the button and ended the call. My father jogging toward my car sent a shock to my heart. "What is it, Dad?"

He leaned over, a tiny bit short of breath. "Phone call for you."

Everything moved in slow motion, like when you know another car is about to hit you. "Who is it?"

"Wouldn't give his name. Just said it was important."

Getting out from the car, my legs felt like gummy worms. Corrigan needed to know about this current call. "Tell the guy to hang on a minute longer."

"You think it's that sicko again?" The sunburst lines around my dad's eyes deepened. "Obscene callers don't ask for someone by name. Or do they? If it is him he's not gonna get a chance to upset you again."

"It's okay, Dad. It's probably a business associate." Every step toward the house reminded me of the last mile a death row inmate takes.

"Hello?"

"Is this Claire DeNardo?" It was my unhappy landlord. He complained about leaving me messages which went unanswered, finally resorting to calling my father's number. "Your rent check was late and when you did submit it, you neglected to sign it."

A deep exhale pushed the fear out of me. An unsigned check was a simple mistake. Nobody would die from it. I promised to remedy the error that same day.

After the call and my explanation, my father's anxious face relaxed.

"Dad, you really need caller ID on this phone. We've talked about it before."

He changed the subject. "Did you find what you needed? You were outside for a while."

"Um hm." My turn to change the subject. "You know, a meatball or two would taste good now." I didn't know if they'd go down okay, but it was important he not think anything happening spooked me. We were just a father and daughter spending time, eating. That's what my family does best anyway.

My father served up the steaming meatballs, wonderful, fragrant orbs of ground veal and pork. We sat down and I cut into one, letting the steam rise. The fork was almost in my mouth when the sound of a motor running stopped it. I sprinted to the living room window, but it was only the beat up truck Mr. Samartano across the street used for business.

My dad poured more *sugo* on his meatballs. "You expecting someone?"

I acted surprised, like my actions had been perfectly normal. "No. Just wondered what that racket was."

"Samartano has had that truck since you were in braces. You forget how loud it was?" He motioned for me to sit back down.

"Guess so." I shoved some of the meatball into my mouth. Still hot, but so good. The next thing I knew, both of them were gone. I wiped the *sugo* from around my mouth and checked the time. *Where was that police car?* Out of my chair again. "Need help with the dishes?"

"What dishes? You heard about this new invention, the dishwasher?"

I smirked and put my index finger to my temple. “I’ve heard of such a thing. Let me use it. It’ll be a new thrill. Go sit.”

Dishes done, I joined him in the living room and stood in front of the picture window, scanning the area. Down the street was an unfamiliar car. I checked my phone. A text from Corrigan told me the unmarked vehicle should have arrived and would stay until the morning. Sighing my relief, I sat down next to my favorite guy.

Twenty more minutes passed before brushing my lips against his cheek. “Have to go see a sick friend. Call you tomorrow. I love you.”

He returned the hug. “Love you too. Hey! Wanna take some meatballs home with you? Maybe give some to your sick friend?”

I left my dad’s place carrying a covered dish of meatballs drenched in marinara.

That roller coaster ride of emotion tired me. Guilt, my frequent companion, took its favorite spot in my head. Lying to my father was the least of it. Putting his wellbeing at risk was unforgiveable.

My next stop would also take its toll. To add to the bad feelings, I planned on disregarding another of Gino’s rules. “Never let the client see you sweat.” If Gino knew how often I broke his rules with Michael, he’d yank me down to Miami. The only investigating I’d be doing there would be on which suntan lotion let the most rays in.

Michael must have heard my car’s roar because he was waiting in his doorway. Seeing him, the recently ingested meatballs settled back down in my stomach. I didn’t want to alarm him so forced myself to set my pace at a casual stroll, stopping a bit away from him and speaking in a measured pace. "Hello, Michael."

He tilted his head and squinted at me. "Hi."

"Can I come in?"

A flash of annoyance passed over his face, but it disappeared so fast I chalked it up to my imagination. "Oh, sorry. Of course. You're always welcome." He placed his arm around me and guided me inside. "Would you like some coffee? Or tea?" He disappeared into the kitchen, returning with two cups of tea and some cookies.

My hands shook, thinking about what to tell him and worrying the tea would spill all over. "Just going to let it cool a bit." I set it down on the coffee table.

He sat across from me and took a sip, but observed me over his cup. "Did you get another call?"

My playacting crumbled into a wobbly mess. "He knew what I did today."

Michael set his cup down and strode over to close the space between us. Bending over he embraced me while I whimpered into his shoulder. He stroked my hair and then my cheek, comforting me with soft murmurs. We remained like that until the uncomfortable truth about us at this time came back to me. I was supposed to be the professional here. He was the client in need. Now with me falling apart, our roles had blurred. If Gino knew about this he would, no doubt, be ripping off his gold chain.

I pulled away and wiped my eyes. "Sorry, Michael. Shouldn't have done that." I picked up the tea cup and took a sip to buy time.

He straightened. "No. My fault."

"You don't need to apologize for things I do." My nose ran and I stood up to find my purse for a tissue. "You're kind and sweet, but you hired me to do a job, not cry on your shoulder." Wiping my nose is never attractive, but it didn't deter Michael, who planted a kiss on my cheek.

"Claire, I don't want anything to happen to you. Ever." He looked down at his feet. "I care very much for you."

Under any other circumstances, his announcement would have made me tingle. But someone had threatened to kill me. I crossed my arms in front as if to protect myself from any more emotions. "Michael, I appreciate what you're saying. But shouldn't we wait to see what happens between us after we find Constance's murderer?" I cringed, hating to hurt his feelings. It was like when, at the age of nine, Vinnie Raselli asked me to go to the grade school dance. When I refused, he cried. My guilt made me change my mind and suffer the humiliation of going with the only boy who was shorter than me.

Michael sat down on the sofa and pulled me next to him. "That's just it. Drop the case. It's too dangerous."

Get off the case. Music to my ears. Let the police do the job. I could be safe, snuggled in Michael's arms. Just that sweet, cozy thought made me want to rearrange his furniture. But Sister Mary Magdalene, my fifth grade teacher, drilled into our still spongy heads that once you start something, finish it. Although she probably didn't mean do something that would be the finish of me.

I gently pulled away from him. "That's out of the question."

He leaned forward. "Then I'm firing you. As of now."

"You can but, Sister Mary Magdalene said—"

"Who?"

"Never mind."

"Invoice me for final payment."

"We'll talk about it after *Cannoli's*."

Ignoring his frown, I excused myself to go freshen up in the bathroom. On the way down the hall, I noticed the door to his study was open. Two desks sat across from each other and were both so neat it was hard to believe anyone ever sat behind either one. A business card, the only object out of place, lay right on the edge of the desk closest to the door. The ivory-colored piece looked ready to drop to the floor, so I stepped into the room to push it further in. One glance at the embossed card and my eyes shot wide open. George Workosky's card. Same as the one Sean had. I shifted my body to pick it up, but all of a sudden, Michael was standing right behind me.

"What are you looking at?"

My hand flew away from the card. "Oh, just how neat this room is." *Yeah, that was a clever cover story.*

Michael didn't skip a beat. "My sister and I shared it. It hasn't been used much since she died." He pointed to the desk with the business card. "This one was hers." His face clouded over for a moment. Then he put his arm around my shoulder, escorted me out of the room, and closed the door behind him.

Chapter Twelve

By the time we arrived at *Cannoli's*, my aunt looked ready to pull her hair out. Short of breath, she said, "Thank God you came early. Place is going crazy." She grabbed two aprons, thrusting them both at me, and rushed back to the front counter.

Michael took one from me. "Looks like it's time to get to work."

We took over the front, and Aunt Lena returned to the kitchen. After thirty minutes or so, she hooked Michael's arm and pulled him away. "We've got some baking to do."

That whole time at *Cannoli's* Michael and I didn't see much of each other, which worked fine for me. Without him around, it was easier to think about Constance's murder and if maybe it would be good for me to back off. Mulling it over, I used my finger to draw a face in the powdered sugar on an empty platter.

Aunt Lena needed help here. It was sure a lot safer and the only thing to fear was weight gain. At least nobody would say, "Too bad Claire's dead. But she did stay slender."

My mind went round and round, like that powdered sugar face, only to reach the same, earlier conclusion. Staying on the case and helping the police was the only way to ensure my safety. Michael would be upset, but he'd get over that once we caught the murderer.

Closing time came after the last customers patted their bellies, exclaimed they shouldn't have eaten all of whatever they'd ordered, and left. Michael still hadn't come out of the kitchen. My aunt had probably had the time of her life with him, discussing cakes and pies and swapping recipes.

I'd begun to clean off the tables when my phone vibrated. Corrigan. Guilt cascaded down my body. I should've gone back to see him after the second phone threat.

Before I could take the call, my aunt roared in. She looked like the abominable snowman, except made of flour. "That boy is a marvel of baking genius. Wait 'til you see what we created. Of course, the honors go to Michael."

Corrigan's call went into voice mail.

Aunt Lena cupped her mouth with one hand and yelled, "Michael, come out and show Claire."

Michael strode out and displayed the most magnificent cake imaginable. At least six layers high, fresh berries covered the top and the edges held chocolate dipped strawberries. Rich-looking dark chocolate dripped down the sides and collided with white swirls and nuts.

Aunt Lena circled him like a ring master at a circus. "Have you ever seen such a beaut?"

My eyebrows shot up to get out of the way of my super-wide open eyes. "It's gorgeous." I half-smiled and winked. "But does it taste as good as it looks?" My mouth watered so much my taste buds put on shower caps.

Michael set it down and my aunt whipped out a knife. Getting the plates and forks was my task. After the initial oohs and ahhs, we ate our own cake slices in silence, savoring each bite. It was so delicious if by myself, I would have used my finger to pick up every last crumb my fork left behind.

When we finished our treat, Aunt Lena clapped her hands like a first grade teacher organizing her young pupils. "Okay you kids, I'll finish cleaning up. You both go. I appreciate your help." She practically shooed us out the door.

We grabbed our stuff and left. My body longed for some sleep. But where?

As if he read my mind, Michael piped up. "My guestroom is still yours."

"Great. But I need to stop home for some things."

"No problem." He bowed at the waist. "It would be an honor to go with you."

After a moment's hesitation, I assented.

To my great relief, my apartment although messy looked undisturbed and, except for Michael and me, empty. I grabbed my necessities for both the night and the next morning, locked up, and we headed out.

First on the agenda at his home was a glass of wine for each of us. No surprise to me, he started up again about the importance of dropping his case. Not on purpose, but I yawned so much it interfered with any meaningful conversation. Stretching as ladylike as possible, my voice thick and sleepy, I said, "We can resume this when I have at least one brain cell awake."

And excused myself to sleep alone.

Before collapsing into bed, I checked my phone for any calls besides that one from Corrigan. My breath caught. Three messages now hung over my head like a pendulum.

The first message came, of course, from Corrigan. "Just checking in to see if you're okay." He paused so long it was surprising he wasn't cut off. "Call me or come to the station. Please." He probably wanted to talk about the call at my dad's and wanted to do it at the station. Maybe he'd found something. Returning his call would be my first priority after hearing the other two.

The second message began. Corrigan again. "Claire, where are you?" No mention of the killer's calls to me. The final message was also from Corrigan. "Claire, pick up." He paused. "Do I have to put out an APB on you? I will if I need to. Call me as soon as you get this."

It was after midnight, but Corrigan did say to call him. My face scrunched up while I punched in the numbers. After a couple of rings, a very sleepy detective answered. "Corrigan here."

My voice went soprano, like it always does when regretting what I just did. "It's me, Claire."

More alert now, he growled. "Where the hell have you been?"

He didn't have to bite my head off. "Just wanted to let you know I'm okay."

"Good. Stay that way."

"I'm trying."

Through a yawn, he added, "Also wanted to let you know the killer used a disposable phone for that second call. Can't trace it." He paused. "And, Claire, don't leave me hanging again. I hate worrying." Before I could respond, he hung up.

Anxiety kept me flipping, awake, from side to side but finally a deep sleep overtook me.

Unfortunately, Ed's call started my morning a lot sooner than I'd have liked. "It's so early." I moaned and rubbed my eyes with my free hand.

He sounded like he'd just taken caffeine intravenously. "Time's awastin'. Wanna talk to you about what I found in Luther's office, or to be more accurate, in his trash can. Meet me at the Owl at six."

I groaned. The thought of greasy spoon aromas made my stomach shrivel. "Can't you tell me now?"

"No can do. Gotta see it."

"Okay, see you at 6:00." I stuck out my lower lip and blew my hair out of my eyes. Another day of sneaking out of Michael's house. You'd think I was a hooker.

I showered, dressed quickly, and opened the bedroom door to the smell of coffee and something made with vanilla. A few steps out of the room stood Michael, holding a cup of tea and a muffin.

"For me?"

He grinned like a kid giving an apple to his favorite teacher. "I heard the shower. Afraid you'd leave without eating something. And we still haven't settled on my final payment."

"Aw, that's so sweet. Only have a few minutes, but then I *do* have to, to…visit my father. We'll discuss the final payment later."

He didn't notice my hesitation. Nor did he question why the visit to my father was so early. Unwilling to tempt fate, though, I stuffed the strawberry cream cheese muffin in my mouth so it would be impossible for me to give any coherent answers.

We said our goodbyes with a quick hug. Cozy and warm from the muffin and hug, I didn't notice the dark blue car until it came up right behind me.

My grip on the steering wheel tightened while keeping the unfamiliar car in my sights. Until it turned off three blocks later. The adrenaline rush left me limp as a linen suit on a sultry day. My nerves were writing their own version of reality. Rotating my neck and dropping my shoulders helped relax me, until I realized what time it was. I hate being late. I'm always worried the other person will leave before I arrive.

Ed had already cleaned his plate when I rushed into the Owl. He leaned back, toothpick in mouth, tapping his foot. "Started to think maybe you weren't gonna show." After he accepted my apology for being tardy, I asked about what he'd found.

"Take a gander." He pulled out a wrinkled and stained yellow stub. "Found this stuck to the bottom of John Luther's trash can. Or should I call him the future CEO and King of Triton? Anyway, he must have thought he got rid of it."

I took the crinkled ticket stub and held it close to my face. It was the kind you get when you valet park. Time stamped just a couple of hours before Constance's death. "Do you think Constance was with him then?"

Ed pointed his index finger at me like it was a gun. "Bingo."

The name of a restaurant was printed on the other side of the ticket. "The Grape. Hmm. Probably worth a visit."

"Want me to tag along?" He grinned. "Maybe twist a few arms?"

"Thanks, but I prefer my questioning non-violent."

Ed was already in too deep. Plus, I needed to stick to the case, to keep it within my grasp. There was little enough within my control, but what there was, I planned to hang on to, especially with those threatening phone calls. It was the only way to keep my sanity. "Besides, you've helped plenty."

He looked like a kid who'd only received raisins while trick-or-treating. "Yeah. Sure. Okay." He stood, stretched, and then headed toward the restaurant door.

I rushed after him. "Hey, Ed. Thank you." My impression was that somehow I'd let him down. "Is it alright to call you when I'm done?"

He pulled out his cigarettes and nodded. "You do that." He shuffled away.

Realizing my question sounded little more than throwing him a bone, I followed him outside. "Ed!" When he turned, I slapped my forehead with the palm of my hand. "Forgot all about the meeting this morning with another client. Do you think you could check with the valets?"

"Easy as pie."

We went our separate ways, and I had just taken a seat behind my office desk when my cell phone rang. "This is Claire DeNardo."

"What do you think you're doing?" Corrigan's words were clipped.

I wanted to quickly disconnect and change my number. "What do you mean?"

"Claire, this isn't a game. You could get hurt, even killed. I don't want that, and I'm guessing neither do you."

I didn't say anything, but my legs bounced up and down so hard they hit the underside of my desk.

After a few seconds of heavy silence, he said, "Meet me at Three Birds Restaurant on Madison Road at 2:00 p.m. today. Do you know where that is?"

My legs stopped twitching. "I'll find it. But why do you want to get together? You should know you can't talk me out of this case. Not now."

He huffed. "We'll see about that."

I stared at the phone after we'd disconnected. Realizing it wouldn't talk back, I set it down and turned on my computer. The phone rang again.

This time though, the call was more than welcome. "Hi, Michael. How are you?" Despite my attempt to sound cheerful, the conversation with Corrigan left its mark.

"Something's wrong, isn't it?" Michael was all concern and caring. "Say the word and I'll be there in a minute. You're at your office, right?"

"Yes. You don't need to come here. It's just…" My voice trailed off while my brain searched for the right explanation. "I'm hungry." That was lame, but I didn't want him to know about my meeting with Ed or that Corrigan wanted me off the case too.

Excitement coursed through Michael's voice. "Then this was the perfect time to call. How does osso bucco with risotto sound for dinner?"

"Irresistible." Anticipation of a meal like that wiped out the nasty taste of the last few nights. "What time is dinner?"

"What about 7:00?"

Enough time to meet with Corrigan, get home, make sure no one was lurking about, change clothes, and get to Michael's."One question though."

He chuckled. "Dessert is crème brulee."

Not only was this sweet man a great cook, he could also read my mind. "Lovely." My dopey smile lingered even after our call ended.

My phone rang again. My father this time.

"Tell me you've given this case up."

"My meeting with the client is tonight," I hedged.

"So you haven't done it yet. Pumpkin, let the cops handle it. That's what they get paid for." He blew out a deep breath. "I hate to interfere with your life. That's what we have Lena for. But I love you, and if something happened to you I'd have to go after the sonofabitch myself."

"I know." I felt like his little girl again. "You won't have to worry any more, okay?" Was fibbing to your father a bigger sin than lying to the police?

"Okay. No more bugging you about it. So, do you wanna go to church with me next Tuesday? I'm having a mass said for your mother."

I hadn't been inside Holy Trinity, or any church for that matter, since my mother died. "Sure, what time?"

"The mass is at 8:00 in the morning, so afterwards, we can get some breakfast. My treat."

Going to mass would make him happy. After that scare with the phone call at his place, I at least owed him that. The cops hadn't seen anything suspicious in their stakeout, but the sooner the killer was caught, the happier and more relieved I'd be.

"Sure, Dad. That sounds nice."

Right after we hung up, a shiver went down my spine, and I recalled one of my uncles telling me it meant someone had just walked on my grave. That reminded me of my meeting later today with Corrigan. Definitely a grave one. I wrinkled my nose at my own bad joke.

Not having heard from Ed yet, I called him on my way to Three Birds Restaurant. Ed's voice mail picked up. A recording of a man who sounded straight out of an old police procedural show spoke. "Put your hands up. You don't have the right to be silent. Leave your name and a message. If you're innocent I'll call you back." I laughed out loud and left him a message to call me.

I got to the restaurant a couple minutes before the designated time, but Corrigan tapped his foot like he'd been waiting hours for me. He actually pulled out my chair for me. I hadn't seen manners like that since my mother signed me up for Holy Trinity's etiquette class.

"Hello, Claire." Corrigan sat down after me, which banished my fear he'd loom over me like a banshee in a bad dream. "Would you like something to drink?"

My mouth was parched, probably from nerves. "Something cold and diet sounds good."

After the waitress took our order, we sat without saying anything. He inspected one of the sugar packets like he'd never seen one, while I glanced around debating whether or not to ask why he wanted me there. He finally broke the silence. "Was your aunt successful with her matchmaking?"

I almost dropped my napkin. Of all the things I'd expected him to say, that wasn't one of them. "Sort of. Well…" I scratched my head and wondered how to tell him almost nothing but make it sound like revealing. "My aunt's biggest hope is for me to be a Josie."

He stopped fiddling with the sugar. "A Josie?"

I grinned. "Yeah, Josie's my aunt's niece, almost like her daughter. Finished high school and got married. One kid, with another on the way. Still madly in love with her husband and vice versa."

He smiled, almost wistfully. "Not a bad life."

I shrugged. "But it's not for everyone."

He rubbed his chin. "No, it isn't. I guess a career fulfills some women."

"Maybe she can have both." Were we were talking about Josie or me?

"A guy would be lucky to find a woman like that."

I pursed my lips. "So, Detective Corrigan, you're looking for a woman who'll bring home a paycheck, raise the kids, and manage to keep the house neat. I suppose you also want her to be a babe."

He raised an eyebrow in amusement. "Call me Brian. And don't get all worked up. I don't want Super Woman. Just a partner in love and marriage." The corners of his lips curled into a mischievous smile. "Of course her being hot wouldn't hurt things."

Our beverages arrived and the conversation stopped for a moment. He took a sip of his coffee and added the contents of the worn packet he'd messed with. "As enjoyable as your company is, I wanted to see you for a different reason."

I took a long sip. "Not interested in my charming ways, huh?" From years of experience in parochial school, I knew when a lecture was coming.

"You're not going to like it, but here it is. I asked you to drop Mr. Adler's case. Now I'm telling you. Stay out of Ms. Tompka's—Mallorie's— murder investigation. You're way too involved and you're interfering with police work."

Of course, he hadn't just wanted to talk about women's roles. I kept my voice low and even. "I have to be involved. Remember? Mallorie died at my door. And don't forget, someone's threatened me and called my father's house. I'm going to keep on—" I bit my hyperactive tongue.

It looked like a small explosion had occurred in Corrigan's eyes. "Keep on what?" Before I could answer he went on. "Keep on the case? When are you going to stop?" He huffed, "When you get the next call? Or will you wait until you get murdered too?"

My natural reaction to any conflict is to sink back and make myself small, but I thought of Michael and my father and sat tall. Sarcasm weaved itself through my next words. "My apology for not going along with what you think is best, but a lot has happened to me and people I care about." I arched my eyebrow. "By the way, you never told me if you had any clues as to who's making those calls to me."

He folded his arms and rested them on the table. "Like I said on the message. They came from disposable phones. Made one call and tossed it. No clues." He leaned in so close we were in danger of bumping noses. "You know, not telling me everything means we could miss something important. Something that could help us solve this case."

He sat back and made his hands into fists, then flexed them open. "And I can't keep you safe if you continue running around with suspects or their accomplices, like Workosky. Understand?"

I gripped the sides of my chair. "How did you know about Workosky? You followed me, didn't you? Oh, never mind. What do you expect me to do? Sit back patiently and hope the police catch the murderer before he makes me victim number three?"

He hissed. "Yes. I don't want you hurt. In fact I hope you'll be around a long, long time." Each of his next words was distinctly enunciated. "But not on this case."

I rubbed my forehead, tired of putting up a brave face. No words could describe my terror of whoever was behind those calls, but the police weren't any further ahead at catching this guy than me. No doubt he might kill me, but if I could get to the murderer before he got to me, I could stop freezing up every time my phone rang. And what did Corrigan mean, hoping I'd be around? Around where? Him? It didn't make any sense. Rather than ask for details though, I just stared down at the table.

"Besides, what would you do if you caught the killer?"

Trying to think of a reasonable answer, I played with my straw. "Hand him over to you?"

He sat back with a satisfied smirk. "Good answer. Then why don't we just remove you, the middleman, and let the police catch him themselves?"

"What if you don't? I'm sure other cases will take precedence."

He slammed his hand down on the table. "I swear to you, we will get this guy. You need to back away. For your own good."

Thinking straight wasn't possible. Neither was staying calm. "I can't." I crossed my arms like a stubborn child.

His jaw tightened. "Okay. I can't force you to drop the case, but be aware; you could be arrested for obstructing justice. In fact, maybe you'd be safer in jail."

Pouring my drink over his head appealed to me, but that'd solve nothing. I controlled my voice. "I'll stay out of your way." I stood up. "Thanks for the tea."

He rose as well. "You're welcome. And, except for

me, don't trust anyone. Including your client."

I froze. "You can't mean Michael? Have you been at this so long you can't recognize the good guys?"

He harrumphed. "I've been at this long enough to know anyone can be a bad guy. Including Michael Adler."

We left the restaurant at the same time, in the same mood. Angry and frustrated. But at least I anticipated a tasty meal. It was petty, but I hoped Corrigan's dinner would be a cold, two-day-old pizza in front of his television. Watching reruns of *Law and Order*.

Outside the restaurant, I drummed on my steering wheel and struggled to calm down. It was clear Corrigan was just doing his job and he didn't want any help. But if he thought even Michael could be a suspect, well then, he was way off. I brushed the memory of that business card away. It'd been on Constance's desk. The card belonged to her and that was that.

Before any niggling thoughts could enter my mind, I checked my phone. Ed hadn't called back. I tried him again, but didn't get any answer. My stomach tied itself up, like it knew something I didn't.

Except for his cell phone number and day job, I didn't know much about Ed, like where he lived, who his friends were, if he had any family. My brows knit and I debated going to The Grape to see if he was there when my phone jingled.

Praise heaven, it was Ed. He sounded like he'd bet everything on the winning racehorse. "Valet was a dead end. Found something a lot better though. On my way to check it out."

My heart fluttered with excitement and fear of the case getting away from me. "Where are you? I'll meet you there."

"No can do. Meet you at your office at…8:00 p.m."

Eight. The same time I was supposed to be at Michael's, but this could be way more important. Maybe dinner could be postponed. Only one way to know.

Michael picked up on the second ring. "Hi, Claire."

"Michael, something's come up. We, rather I, might have an important breakthrough in Constance's case."

He sucked in a deep breath. "What?"

"I'm really sorry, but, um, they're meeting me at my office this evening." I cringed, picturing his disappointment.

He didn't say anything but I felt as if I'd eaten lamb chops at a PETA meeting. "Can you hold off dinner until tomorrow night?"

"Sure. But aren't you giving up the case?" I could hear his impatience rising. "We'd agreed. Didn't we?"

"Um, we didn't actually come to an agreement…" I hedged. "We'll discuss it tomorrow at dinner. Okay?"

"What will it take to persuade you?"

He was upset, but I certainly wasn't looking for an argument. "Michael, sorry, another call's coming in." There wasn't one, but I didn't need another lecture. It was already hard enough keeping myself from hiding under my bed with the dust bunnies until this whole thing blew over.

I'd gotten to my office early, but it was now 8:15 and still no sign of Ed. I waited, tapping a pen against my keyboard. For a man who was always on time, this didn't seem right. Then came some grunts and several loud thumps outside my door. I shoved my phone in my pocket and zoomed out of my office. Just in time to witness Ed's last roll down the stairs.

Chapter Thirteen

I gasped. His legs were twisted at the wrong angles. Blood covered his white shirt, probably from the huge gash on his forehead. His eyes were closed; his chin jutted out and rested on the last step. I raced down the stairs and almost tripped before reaching him, catching a glimpse of someone's back as they fled. With only the streetlamp to help me, I couldn't get a good look at Ed's attacker.

Ed's labored breathing meant he was alive. Badly hurt, but alive. My hands were slippery either from blood or my own nervous perspiration because I dropped my phone, picked it up again and dialed 911. As we waited for the ambulance, I reassured Ed he'd be fine. He'd passed out by then, so the comforting was for me.

By the time the ambulance arrived, my legs were stiff from kneeling beside Ed and I was near hysteria. The EMTs worked efficiently and loaded Ed up to go to the hospital. It was then a crumpled piece of cardstock paper came into view. It must have fallen from Ed's hand and then he tumbled on top of it. I stooped and picked it up. Too bad the top part had been ripped off; it was indecipherable.

As if by magic, Corrigan appeared and, donning gloves, whisked the note away from my fingers and handily dropped it into an evidence bag. I opened my mouth to protest, but realized it'd do no good. He pocketed the bag without examining it and asked, "Are you okay, Claire?"

I wiped a tear away with the back of my hand. "What do you think?"

"That you need some time away from this office and this case." He paused a moment. "Are you up to answering some questions?"

The hallway and downstairs crawled with police. "Yes, but not here. You'll have to ask me at the hospital. I've got to be sure Ed's all right. It's my fault…whatever happened to him is entirely my fault." My chest felt tight realizing it had been easy enough for me to put Ed's life in danger. Yet I hadn't even bothered learning anything about that life.

Corrigan nodded. "Go ahead and lock up your office. I'll take you to the hospital. If he regains consciousness, I'll need to speak with him." He took out his notepad again. "Do you know his next of kin? Or someone else to notify?"

I shook my head, feeling too ashamed to speak.

Corrigan employed his siren, and we arrived at the hospital before I'd have been able to pull out of my parking space. He opened my door to help me out, but my legs felt weak and were as useless as a unicycle in the Tour de France bike race.

"Don't know if I can even stand."

He leaned in. "Then slide out and hold on to me."

For just a moment I draped myself on to him like an

expensive coat. Feeling uneasy though, I gamely stood on my own. Although still a bit wobbly, my legs managed to hold me.

Inside the hospital, Corrigan took charge and flashed his credentials. Dr. Gupta, the ER physician visited us in the waiting room. He shook his head and looked solemn. "Mr. Horwath is still unconscious. He has three broken ribs, a fractured leg, a ruptured spleen, and numerous lacerations. Our biggest concern, though, is his skull fracture. There's been some hemorrhaging. He's in surgery right now." He assured us someone would be back to give us an update after the operation and excused himself.

I held it together until Dr. Gupta left. Then the only way to stop from whimpering was to stuff my hand in my mouth. "My fault. All my fault." I fell back into a chair and dropped my head into my hands. Guilt, regret, and fear all passed through me, each boring a separate hole in my spirit.

Corrigan pulled a chair next to me and handed me his handkerchief. After gaining some self-control, I sat up and looked at the lipstick and mascara-stained piece of cloth, wondering if he'd even want it back.

It took me a moment before trusting myself to speak. "Ed told me he'd found something important about Constance's murder. He wanted to show it to me. But then…" A tear rolled down my cheek and I dabbed at it with the crumpled handkerchief. "Someone attacked him." Another tear followed.

Corrigan covered my icy hand with his warm one. "I realize this is hard for you, but it isn't your fault. It's the fault of the scumbag who attacked him." He watched me, waiting for that idea to sink in. Then, "Can you handle a few more questions?"

My head bobbed once in reply.

"You stated you saw someone running away. Can you describe that person at all?"

"It was too dark and I was focusing on Ed. Sorry I'm not a better witness."

"You're doing fine. Something else may come to you later." Corrigan reached into his pocket and pulled out the plastic bag with the paper Ed had dropped. He held it up to me. "There's not much left of it, but do you have any idea what this says or why it's important?"

I tilted my head until my nose was practically against the bag. "Looks like a piece of a business card, although it's hard to tell what it used to say. Sorry." My fingertips pressed against my lips. "Sorry, I keep saying sorry."

We'd sat there for thirty minutes more, with Corrigan asking questions, most of which I couldn't answer. When a uniformed policeman approached us, Corrigan motioned for the cop to meet him outside the waiting room. They spoke too softly for me to hear. After a brief conversation between the men, Corrigan handed the plastic evidence bag to the officer.

He returned and, without my asking, explained, "Officer Joblonsky is taking the evidence to the lab. They may at least be able to lift some fingerprints. That'll give us a place to start."

A phone rang and I jumped a bit, like someone had laid one of those trick hand buzzers under my rear. It reminded me. "What about Ed's phone? Maybe we can find out who he talked to before he got attacked."

"Way ahead of you, Claire. We checked. No phone on him. And what do you mean by 'we'? You're out of this, especially now."

"Ed's in here because of me." I poked myself in the chest. "I'm responsible for this and now I have to see it through."

Corrigan ran his fingers through his hair. Through gritted teeth he said, "Then there's no guaranteeing your safety. God knows, though, I don't want you to be the next one on a gurney."

Adrenalin gone, I slumped in my chair. "Me either, but quitting would mean letting Michael and now Ed down. Please understand that."

His jaw muscles worked and I expected him to reprimand me and maybe even arrest me like he'd threatened. Instead he nodded. "Yeah, I understand, but think about it. Two murders, threats, and one assault. Do you really think you'd be able to handle this guy if you found him?"

I wrung my hands, afraid of the truth. A gun might change the answer. Promising myself to get one tomorrow, I said, "Yes." Then shut up, before my brainless tongue added, 'I hope.'

He straightened the lapels on his suit. It was that or throttle me. Once in control of his temper he said, "At least move to a different office." He stood, preparing to walk away.

Instead of a snappy comeback, "You're not leaving me, are you?" leapt out of my mouth. I bit my tongue to punish it.

He turned around. "Just to stretch my legs." A smile crept onto his face, but he squelched it right away. "You want me to stay here with you?"

"Well…yes…." It was late and obviously my mouth, instead of my brain, had taken on the night shift. He cocked his head while I stared at the floor, trying to compose a response slippery enough to avoid admitting I needed his company.

A nurse approached us, rescuing me. “Mr. Horwath is out of surgery, but he’s still unconscious and in critical condition.”

Corrigan shot an empathetic glance my way, then turned back to the nurse and said, “Thank you. An officer will be posted outside his room. He can let us know when Mr. Horwath is awake.”

With the nurse gone, Corrigan volunteered to take me home. “You could use some rest.”

I must’ve given him a look like Ichabod Crane facing the Headless Horseman because he added, “I could sleep on your couch until the morning if you’d feel safer that way. We can pick your car up from the office tomorrow. You probably shouldn’t drive tonight.”

My first reaction was to decline, visualizing how messy my apartment was. Rational thought finally broke through. Without someone around tonight, I’d never get any rest. Barging in on Michael so late would be inexcusable. I bit my lower lip, and issued my warning. “You could sleep on my couch, but it’s not real comfortable. And there’s no coffee to drink in the morning.”

He suppressed a smirk. “On the force, you learn to sleep anywhere. Don’t worry about the coffee.”

I stood too fast and felt all the blood rush to my feet. To keep from passing out, I dropped my head down and shut my eyes.

Corrigan put his hands on my shoulders. “Are you okay?”

I looked up and realized he had a nice nose, masculine and sort of regal. Funny what you notice during a murder investigation. "Yes."

He dropped his hands. "Good. Shall we go?" He offered me his arm. "Might be a good idea to lean on me."

We parked at my apartment, and Corrigan pulled out his gun. "Don't get out until I say so, okay?" He scanned the parking area. Once he determined it was safe, he helped me out of the car.

After making sure my apartment was all clear, he settled in, and I excused myself to my own bed. Since taking on this case, two different men had spent the night with me. Of course, they'd been asleep in other rooms. I'd have found that humorous if terror of being the next victim or guilt over Ed didn't use up all my emotion.

Once in bed, I flopped from side to side but couldn't find a comfortable spot. Deciding a drink of water would help me sleep I cracked my bedroom door and stuck my head out. No Corrigan, not on the sofa or anywhere else in the room. "Brian?"

I sucked in air as my heart rose into my throat and threatened to choke me. Wild, irrational thoughts raced through my mind. The killer got Corrigan and I was next.

Fighting the urge to crawl out my bedroom window, I tiptoed into the living room and grabbed a paperweight from the hall table to throw at the killer. I hadn't dazzled anyone as the girls' junior league third baseman but maybe raw terror would improve my throw. Dismissing my worst-case-scenario thoughts, I crept a few steps forward and heard water running in the kitchen. My arm dropped and I blew out a shaky breath, realizing how ridiculous my reaction had been. There'd been no assault. Corrigan had been thirsty and went into the kitchen for something to drink.

I backed away, not wanting him to see me standing there in my white cotton nightgown covered with smiling pink alligators, ready to throw what was no more effective than a rock.

Two steps closer to my room, my phone rang.

Every other noise stopped and the phone's ring resounded, like an old grandfather clock in a haunted mansion. My face felt hot. It was probably the same color as the alligators on my nightgown.

Corrigan rushed out of the kitchen and picked up my phone. He handed it to me, the muscles in his jaw tightening. I frantically shook my head as if he'd asked me to hold a cobra. He hit the speaker button and pushed the phone in my face, giving me no choice.

The throaty hushed voice didn't sound like mine. "Hello?"

A woman on the other end slurred her words, like maybe a few drinks guided her number-pressing finger. "Is Kenneth there?"

Corrigan moved his hand across his throat. Either he meant for me to end the call or he wanted me to slice him up. I went with the first. "No. Wrong number."

She giggled. "So sorry."

I ended the call and pitched the phone onto the sofa next to me. Twisting, I fell back, right on top of it. *Smooth move*. I dug the phone out from under my behind.

Corrigan sat down next to me. "Too bad it wasn't the killer."

I sat up straight. "What d'ya mean, too bad?"

"Don't get upset. Just meant I'd have been able to listen in. Maybe pick up on something you've missed."

"Oh, that's right. While I'm a mess of nerves, you,

Detective Cool-As-An-Ice-Cube with your mighty skills, could figure out who the murderer is by merely listening to his voice." I crossed my arms and became aware that my only piece of clothing was a thin cotton alligator-covered nightgown. The heat of embarrassment rose up though me, like being a chicken on a rotisserie. God and everybody could see through to my everything. I tightened my arms around my body and stood up.

"Excuse me." His eyes followed me as I marched into my bedroom and replaced the nightgown with jeans and a huge flannel shirt.

Corrigan cleared his throat when I returned. I could've sworn it was to cover up a chuckle. His voice turned serious, concerned. "Did you want me? Before the call. I mean, were you looking for me?"

"Couldn't sleep." I yawned and stretched. "Maybe if we watch some TV it'll help relax me." I picked up the remote and sat down. Corrigan joined me, and we flipped through channels until coming to an old *I Love Lucy* episode.

***

When morning came, my head was on Corrigan's shoulder and his was on top of mine. He was still snoring softly. Cozy, except he was the cop and I was potentially the future victim. Besides, the bathroom called to me. Holding my breath, I eased my head out from under his. He stirred a bit, but his head flopped backwards onto the top of the sofa and he resumed snoring.

I showered, threw on an old fleece robe hanging in the bathroom, and stepped out to see if Corrigan was still under the Sandman's influence. He was awake, sitting up and rubbing his neck.

"Would you like something for your stiff neck,

Detective?"

He winced as he stretched out. "A massage?" he asked, with a mischievous smile.

"No. I was thinking more along the lines of Advil."

Through a yawn he said, "Careful, you know what we do to drug pushers. And call me Brian."

I held out two capsules. "Well, Brian, do you want some milk to wash them down?"

While he swallowed and grimaced, my phone rang. I reached for it and, once I realized who the caller was, hoped Corrigan would keep quiet. Michael didn't need to know the detective and I were together so early in the morning.

"Hi, Michael." My effort to keep my voice normal failed. Even to me it sounded strained.

Corrigan's eyebrows shot up, and he made it obvious he planned on eavesdropping.

"Claire. Sorry for calling so early, but what did you find out?"

My mind went blank. With everything that had gone on last night, there had been no time to prepare what to say. So I stalled. "Why don't we talk about it tonight?" Before he could object, I added, "I was just on my way out for an 8:00 appointment. Then another at 10:00. After that, there's …verifying the tip about your sister's case." I crinkled my nose. My lies left me with a bad taste. Corrigan hearing them made it worse.

Michael sighed. "Okay. You'll still be here tonight at 8:00?" He sounded peeved, but it couldn't be helped. He'd be over it once I explained it all away with more fabricated excuses.

Withholding information to a client, especially Michael, was inexcusable, but I had to get my head around what happened to Ed and why. Once accomplished, of course, I'd tell him. Afterwards, he might not even be as anxious to get me to drop the case.

Corrigan's eyes found mine. He had a wide open grin on his face. "My, how easy stretching the truth comes to you."

I blushed like the first time I got fitted for a bra. "It's only to protect him from…from…"

Any previous merriment dropped from Corrigan's face. "From knowing everything about the case?" His eyebrows knitted. "You don't completely trust him either, do you?"

I looked away. "That's not true. Hey, I better put some decent clothes on so you can take me back to my car." I spun away before he could say another word.

We filled his car with small talk. When he pulled into the office parking lot, he asked me again if I'd be okay. "Um hmm. Thanks."

"Whatever you're planning to do today, don't. That is, don't do anything risky. Or stupid. And keep your phone on and close to you."

My eyebrows shot up. "Stupid?" although, as a matter of fact, most of my actions concerning this case fell into that category.

He waved my question away. "You know what I mean."

I took on a country bumpkin accent. "Aw shucks, Sheriff, I reckon I kin manage not to stand behind a kickin' mule."

His lips twitched, almost into a smile, but he turned it into a scowl. "Okay, okay. I'll call you later."

After he dropped me off, my first stop was danger-free enough to please even Corrigan. It was *Cannoli's*, to ask Aunt Lena if she would check in with my dad. A twinge of guilt plucked at me. I should've done that after the last call, but with everything else going on, it got pushed to the back of my mind. But talking to my aunt could fix that. Tell her he mentioned he didn't see her enough. He'd kill me for that, but I'd rather he get annoyed than something happen to him.

Despite it being early, *Cannoli's* hopped with customers. Before I could do more than kiss Aunt Lena's cheek, she handed me an apron and asked me to take the counter for a few minutes until her sometime counter help, all-the-time friend, Angie, arrived. "She was supposed to be here already. Hope her car didn't break down again."

"Okay, but there's something —"

She pinched my cheeks and in a voice you'd use to address a puppy said, "You're such a good kid." We heard the back door open and my aunt tilted her head. "That's probably Angie. Hold your thought." She dashed off to the kitchen.

While I waited, a customer bought a dozen chocolate chunk biscotti. I reached for one for myself, but the phone rang. And rang. Since my aunt didn't answer it, I did.

Heavy breaths, like the caller had been running. Then he began to sing, the tune again different.

"Last night, last night
You saw what I will do.
You're digging way too deep piggy. Oh,
Next time there may not be a warning
And what then will become of you?"

Chapter Fourteen

The call ended, but it took a minute for my arm to move and drop the phone from my ear. Another minute for me to think straight. Struggling for a breath, my eyes scanned the room full of women. He could see me, observe my actions, but the reverse wasn't true. My hand grabbed at my throat and it struck me how this monster had invaded my life and now that of my family's. I wanted to whisk myself and my family away someplace else, but capturing this guy was the only way we'd ever be safe.

Turning my back to the customers, I called Corrigan to have a breakdown, but it went into his voicemail. I didn't leave a message, though because Angie came right up to me, tying her apron around her waist. "Go on, Sweetie. I got this." So intent on taking care of the next customer, she didn't notice my state.

"Thanks." If this were an ordinary day, I would've gone into the kitchen for goodbyes. This time was different. My aunt would have picked up on my traumatized state in less time than it takes a flea to jump on a dog.

I started toward my car to drive to the police station, but stopped halfway there. *That song.* Again it was a familiar one, but placing it proved impossible for me. Would knowing the names of the songs make it easier to identify the killer? I headed to my office to play some tunes.

Playing song after song in my office yielded nothing, but I'd return to the task after a visit to the hospital. Even if they didn't let me see Ed, I needed to be there for him.

All the way there I checked my rearview mirror to see if someone was following me. Eventually my grip loosened on the steering wheel. No one on the road seemed the least bit interested in my comings and goings.

People around the hospital entrance were greeted by my stomach's growls so I dashed into the coffee shop and grabbed a muffin. It tasted like chocolate-scented Styrofoam. At least it'd keep my belly from announcing its presence to everyone.

I finished the muffin and stepped out of the elevator on Ed's floor. The last bite stuck in my throat, but it stopped bothering me when I spotted Corrigan.

The detective was pounding one fist into the palm of his other hand. He leaned into a young cop, who looked like he'd rather be anywhere but in front of Corrigan.

The infraction must have been serious, judging from Corrigan's reaction. Something to do with Ed? Had Ed died? I froze. Being confronted with bad news can do that to me. Before I could thaw, the detective spotted me.

"Claire." The other cop slinked away. "I was going to call you. Ed regained consciousness for a little bit." He clenched his fists. "He slipped back though." His voice rose, "Officer Johnson notified me too late."

Without thinking, I clutched Corrigan's arm. "Did Ed say anything?"

"Nurse said he tried, but couldn't get any words out."

I templed my hands over my nose and mouth. Tears filled my eyes. Corrigan lowered his voice and between gritted teeth said, "I'll catch the bastard, I promise."

I sniffed, "But that won't help Ed now."

Corrigan stared at me for a second and chewed on his lower lip. "Come on." He took my elbow.

I stood cemented to the floor. "Where to?"

"Cafeteria. You look like you could use a cup of something."

The muffin left a lump in my throat. Maybe some tea would wash it down, but I didn't want to miss out if Ed regained consciousness. Corrigan must have read my mind. "Everyone on this floor now knows if there's any change in Ed's status, they better get hold of me immediately."

We rode down the elevator side by side. It's funny how everyone stares straight ahead when they're riding up or down. But I rebelled and leaned against the wall to check the people getting on and off. Could any of them be the killer, biding their time, waiting to finish Ed off if he did regain consciousness? I shook my head slightly to dislodge that thought. Seeing killers everywhere would render me useless. Not that I'd done any sort of bang-up job so far.

I sighed so loudly, Corrigan and an elderly woman using a walker turned toward me. The woman asked me in a thick Polish accent, "You okay, young lady?"

"Oh yes. Just thinking."

She looked at me through eyes filmy with cataracts and smiled. "I wish for you the thoughts are of joy, not sadness." Her face dropped and her jowls trembled. I wanted to reach out to her, to say something comforting. But the elevator dinged and the doors opened. She set her walker over the gap and turned and pointed her finger first at me and then at Corrigan. "Be good to each other. Too soon life is over."

The door closed. Corrigan cleared his throat and played with his tie. I took his actions to mean he thought being linked with me romantically would be worse than getting caught on video mooning the Pope."There are worse things, you know," I snapped.

He looked straight ahead. "Worse than what?"

"Being, you know, with me." My pride pushed the point.

The corners of his mouth curved upwards. "It's crossed my mind."

The elevator bounced to a stop and the doors opened. I dropped my hands on my hips. "So I've got to guard myself against more than just the killer."

He chuckled.

Together at the cafeteria table, I wrapped my hands around the hot cup of tea and looked down into the liquid. "I got another call this morning at my aunt's restaurant."

He slammed his cup down and the coffee sloshed onto the table."When were you—never mind. Tell me about it."

I did my best with the description. "He sang it again. Different tune, just as familiar though." My voice trembled.

"Could you recall the song?"

"Not without hearing it again." Not sure, even then. That's me, about as useful as a fork with a bowl of soup.

I rested my chin in my hand, my eyes closed, trying to get the tune from my memory down to my mouth. I opened my eyes and shook my head. "Nothing."

"Maybe it'll come back to you. We'll trace the call, although he probably used another disposable phone. Guy must have a dozen. But right now all we've got is a bunch of leads that don't go anywhere. Eagleton is still a person of interest, but we still don't have enough to arrest him." He tapped his spoon against the saucer. "Ed's the best chance we've got."

I pushed back my chair. "Speaking of Ed, I'm going back. I want to be there if he wakes up."

But there was no change and after waiting around for another hour, I decided more good would come from my office work. I reassured myself that things just seemed beyond my fingertips, but if I worked hard enough, the killer's identity would come to me. With luck he'd be captured before he got to me. That feeling of someone walking on my grave overcame me again.

In the hospital parking lot, a teenage girl walked behind me, singing, and paying little attention to her surroundings. I halted so abruptly she almost crashed into me. "What are you singing?"

She pulled out one of her ear buds and, her voice dripped with you-are-an-idiot sarcasm. "OhMyGod, you're like the last person on earth to not know *West Side Story*. It's old, but so good. I'm playing Maria at school. They just did it at the Playhouse a month or so ago." Looking up and shaking her head, she put her ear buds back in and walked away, singing.

My first reaction was to run back and tell Corrigan, but I changed my mind. After all, this was still my case.

Back in my office, the soundtrack to *West Side Story* played on my computer. Sure enough, three of the songs had been used by the killer, *Maria, Tonight* and *America*. Despite the words being very different, listening to the tunes again made my heart race. I'd heard enough.

The guy liked musicals, or he liked that one. How to use this information, though. It wasn't like I could ask Eagleton or Sean or anyone if they happened to enjoy *West Side Story*.

The teenager claimed the Playhouse had done it recently. A quick search of its season offerings revealed *West Side Story* had played only one night. If luck was with me, they kept a record of who had attended.

I called the Playhouse box office and a woman answered. "Hello," I began in my most professional voice. "This is Claire DeNardo, investigator. I'm looking for some information on a recent crime."

The woman's voice rose. "We aren't in some trouble are we? And who did you say you were with?"

Having been told more than once my voice sounded like a child over the phone, and not wanting this woman to think this was a prank call, I spoke in a low tone. "I'm working with the police, and we need the list of those who purchased tickets for *West Side Story*." I squeezed my eyes closed and held my breath.

"Sorry, but that information isn't readily available." She didn't sound sorry at all. "Perhaps if you come in person with the police, we can get it for you."

So much for using my official voice.

Today had zipped by and I realized if I didn't hurry, Michael would be having dinner without me. My stomach, elated it was getting some attention, growled its appreciation. It'd been upset since that dried-out muffin incident this morning.

I threw on some makeup while driving to his house, knowing there'd be delicious food and great company. After the last couple of days, this dinner would be like uncovering a piece of chocolate in a kale salad.

I waited for Michael to come to the door, still unsure what to tell him regarding last night, only knowing to keep Ed out of it. If Michael knew what'd happened to Ed, for sure he'd fire me from the case. This evening was not going to include an argument with Michael.

When he opened the door, wonderful cooking aromas wafted around him. “Hi Claire. Come in.”

“Hi Michael. M-m-m, it smells so good in here.” I commanded my salivary glands to behave so I wouldn’t drool.

He smiled. “Hope you’ll like it. Some wine?”

I returned his smile. “With that aroma, how could I not? And wine would be nice.”

He left the room to pour our drinks, and I glanced around the living room, absently wondering if he had *West Side Story’s* soundtrack. My head throbbed. So what if he did have the soundtrack? Probably thousands of people do, including my father.

“Headache?” Michael returned with two glasses and handed one to me.

“Oh, no. Just…” Better to change the subject. “How about a toast?”

“Okay. To what?”

To finding the killer? “To a wonderful meal and a gracious host.” We raised our glasses.

Dinner was a flurry of mouthwatering food and witty conversation. All of it on Michael’s part. Instead of relaxing me and allowing my charm to dazzle, the wine made me slightly nauseated. I knew there was cause for concern when even a chocolate crème brulee didn’t send me into nirvana. My mind kept going back to the phone calls.

As soon as etiquette allowed, I excused myself to

check my messages. No Corrigan. *Now who was being elusive, damn him.* Slipping my phone into my pocket, I headed to the kitchen and counted my blessings that Michael hadn't brought the case up during dinner. Just a matter of time though before the subject came up. Sure enough, a short time after entering the kitchen, I felt like the turkey who was invited for Thanksgiving dinner.

"Michael, that was such a fantastic meal, the least I can do is help you clean up." My hope was he wouldn't bring up my resigning from the case until much later, if at all.

He half-smiled and handed me a towel. "No argument from me." If only he wouldn't argue with me about anything tonight. My current fragile composure might not have withstood any sort of challenge.

Maybe he sensed that because we worked in companionable silence until everything was cleaned and stored. Without asking, Michael then poured both of us more wine. "You've been so tense. Let's sit down and you can tell me what you learned."

The moment of half-truths had come. No more stalling on this discussion. My mind created and edited what information I was willing to share as Michael guided me to the sofa.

My sin-of-omission report to Michael began with, "The last person to have been with Constance may have been John Luther, Triton's future CEO. She was having an affair with him. Eagleton, her previous lover, and his assistant, Sean Lawrence, knew about it."

Michael sat on the edge of his seat. "Go on."

"Eagleton and Sean Lawrence met with someone from another drug company, a pharmacist named George Workosky, the evening Mallorie was killed."

"Isn't there more? Didn't you tell me someone was bringing you evidence?"

The best way to handle this was with complete dishonesty. "I thought so too. But they never showed up."

Michael's eyes became slits and he folded his arms across his chest. "What aren't you telling me?"

My hand flew to my breast like his question shocked me when, in reality, I would have been surprised if he hadn't asked it. My charade continued. "Michael, how could you think I'm withholding information? You're my client."

He took my hand into his two warm ones. "Sorry. I'm just anxious to get whoever killed Constance. This must be confusing you. One minute I ask you to drop the case; the next I'm asking for information."

"It's okay." My phone vibrated. As much as I wanted to answer it, doing so might mean Michael would learn about my latest threatening call or about Ed. I withdrew my hand and patted his. "Now if you'll excuse me, I have to go to, well, you know." I sprinted to the bathroom as if in competition with five other women for a restroom single-seater.

I closed the bathroom door behind me and checked my phone. One missed call. I called Corrigan back.

"Corrigan here. What's up?"

With my back to the door, I cupped my hand over the phone and whispered, "The tunes are from *West Side Story*. I tried to get a list of who'd seen it at the Playhouse, but they wouldn't give it to me."

"*West Side Story*? Like, 'When you're a Jet— "

"Yeah, that one."

"Not sure I follow you. What does the Playhouse have to do with it?"

"The play was there last month. Maybe the tunes stuck in the killer's head." Now that my theory was out in the open, the intelligence of my assumption seemed doubtful. But he surprised me.

"A long shot, but one worth checking out."

"Count me in on it since it was my idea." I felt like the kid no one likes, but they play with him because he owns the ball.

Corrigan heaved a loud, annoyed sigh. "Tell you what. I'll let you know if I need you."

"But—" He'd disconnected. "What a weasel."

Although unprepared to discuss dropping the case with Michael, I couldn't very well crawl out the bathroom window to avoid it. How wonderful it would be if he realized his thinking was erroneous and begged me to keep digging. But this was Cleveland, not Fantasyland. Like a soldier going into a skirmish, I stood straight, threw my shoulders back and marched out the door.

Michael waited for me in the living room. "Since you

haven't gotten any further on it, do you agree now to drop the case?"

I pretended to have something in my left eye and blinked furiously, even pulling on my eyelid to give me some time. But with my limited acting ability and fear of actually injuring my eye, I stopped stalling. "Do you really, really believe the police can find the murderer, Michael?"

"My faith in them isn't the point here. They haven't been getting threatening calls. The simple truth is my feelings for you have grown and keeping you out of harm's way is now a high priority for me." He paused. "I have a blank check for you. Just tell me what my balance is."

The words came to me all of a sudden, and they managed to follow one of Gino's rules. "Only tell the client what you want him to know."

"If you really want me to back off the case, then so be it. Keep your check, though." My hand rose to block his protest. "Let me finish. Once the police arrest Constance's murderer, you can pay me. I just couldn't take the money before then. Besides, you've already covered my expenses with your initial payment."

Dropping the case wasn't really an option. Now that the killer had touched my family, my only option was see this to the end. A PI can't function if she's scared to distraction that her father and aunt could come to some harm. My intentions were good. Keep everyone important to me as safe and worry-free as possible.

Backing off, therefore, could mean a number of things, including proceeding with more caution. That was my interpretation in this instance.

I forced myself to return his gaze and not to twitch, and in return, he stopped staring at me.

"All right, Claire. We have a deal. By the way, Detective Corrigan wants to see me."

"Maybe he has some information." Skirting an argument tired me out so much my bones ached. "Michael, it's bad form to eat and run, but I'm exhausted. The evening's young, but right now I don't feel like I am. Mind if I head home?"

"Of course not. You've been working so hard. Before you go though, let me give you a massage. It'll relax you."

Ordinarily, I'd give my lifetime membership to Dates4U for a great massage. But right now it wouldn't pay to get relaxed and do something I'd regret later on. So, with much reluctance I declined.

He walked me to the door and placed his arms around my waist, pulling me in to him. "Next time, please stay."

His request was sweet, but it didn't do anything for me. Probably just too wrung out. Still, I responded with a weak smile.

Lost in thought and yawning, I pulled out of the driveway, blind to the parked car and the driver inside it, watching me.

Chapter Fifteen

About five hundred feet from Michael's driveway, Corrigan sat in his car, window down. He waved for me to pull up next to him. I cursed under my breath then worried he'd figured out what I'd just muttered about his heritage.

Taking to heart the saying about the best defense, I rolled my window down. "Why are you following me?"

Instead of responding to my question, he leaned over, opened the passenger's side door for me and growled, "Get in."

He must have observed Michael and me in a less-than-professional stance. Panic spread through my brain and sped up my heart. In all probability, my face took on the expression of someone who'd bitten into an apple and seen half a worm. My fingers felt fat and clumsy as I turned off the ignition and opened my door. The light from a streetlamp brightened the interior a bit, but it was still night.

Corrigan didn't even look at me when I slid into his

car. Not that it would've mattered. God knows why, but he had on sunglasses, making it impossible to read his eyes. "Tailing you wasn't my intention. I wanted to see Adler, but saw a whole lot more." He gritted his teeth. "Why didn't you tell me this case had gotten more personal?"

"Wasn't your business."

"That's where you're wrong. If it affects the case, it's my business." He raised his shades and his eyes flashed. "You don't listen. Anyone could be the killer."

"So, be suspicious of everyone?" I smiled sweetly. "That would mean I shouldn't even trust you." *Could I get jail time for mouthing off to a cop?*

"That's not what I meant and don't try to skate out of this." The muscles in his jaw tensed. "No detective, private or police should get involved with..." His voice trailed off and he blinked. "That is, don't get your feelings tangled..." He glanced away and in a gruff voice concluded, "Don't go liking Adler too much."

"He's a great guy." Crossing my arms, I asked, "Now, why were you following me?"

He tapped his fingers against the steering wheel. "Once again, this visit was to see Adler. But after what I've observed, it might be smart to follow you. Make sure you don't get into trouble."

"And I should be grateful for that?"

By way of an answer, he let out a soft snort. "By the way, I checked on who saw *West Side Story*." He wore a satisfied grin. "Eagleton and his wife."

My eyebrows rose and my mouth formed an 'O'. "Best news I've had in a while."

"It may be something, maybe not. We'll just have to see."

His lack of enthusiasm, real or feigned, frustrated me. "It's more than you had. Can't you at least bring him in for more questioning?"

"Are you trying to tell me how to run this investigation?" By the measured tone of his question, I must have treaded on his ego.

"No, of course not. Only…" My voice rose until it disappeared and I scooted just a bit closer to the door.

"I know. We both want this case solved, but getting ahead of ourselves won't help."

"You're including me?" Had I finally gotten through to him?

He grumbled, "A slip of the tongue. Don't think I've changed my mind about wanting you off this case."

I chewed my upper lip for a moment, thinking. "What about putting Eagleton in an audio lineup. You know, I listen to five guys, each singing a threat."

He shook his head. "Wouldn't do any good. Even a rookie public defender could point out you've already heard Eagleton talk. He'd claim prejudice." Corrigan cleared his throat. "Anyway, you'd be wise to keep your client as just that. A client." His lip curled as he added, "It's hard to keep professional prospective if your body's draped all over him."

Even if he was right about Michael, it wasn't

necessary for Corrigan to follow me everywhere, jutting his nose into my doings. I had Aunt Lena for that.

Holding one hand at my heart, the other hand up like a school guard's, my voice turned solemn. "This shall serve as my pledge to use extreme caution when choosing with whom to associate." I lowered my hands. "Now can you stop following me? Oh, that's right. You weren't."

He leaned back in his seat. "That's right. You just happened to be here, which was an added bonus."

My heart started to do a flip "*Really?*" I almost gushed how good it was to see him too, until he smirked.

"Saved me some time. I could interview him again and keep an eye on you."

My girlish ego shriveled. "So pleased to make your job more convenient."

His expression softened. "Have to admit though. The best part is seeing you."

My insides turned as mushy as the ricotta inside a cannoli. "Yeah." Lame, but it was all I could manage to say. We sat there for a moment with me feeling as awkward as the first time I ate in public with my mouth full of braces.

He cleared his throat and murmured, "Better get on to business. Don't want Adler to notice us talking here together." I nodded and reached for the door handle, but he placed a firm hand on my arm. "Be careful. We don't know who we're dealing with."

That comment was a great flame of passion douser.

"I'm not stupid."

His mouth curved into a smile, showing that cute dimple of his. "No, but you're innocent."

Next came my oh-so-snappy comeback. "That's what you think." Pushing open the door, I stomped back to my car, got in and floored it. It was in reverse, though. Slamming on the brakes, I didn't dare glance over at Corrigan, imagining him laughing.

I stewed at the traffic light a block from Michael's home, tapping my fingers against the steering wheel. Corrigan had no right to be charming one minute then all business the next.

When the light turned green, my thoughts of him switched off. A more urgent issue arose: where to lay my head down and sleep. Returning to my apartment without a scout checking for any unwanted visitors didn't appeal. My office was more a crime scene than a safe harbor. Couldn't crash at my dad's without the worry of bringing more danger to him. Aunt Lena was out. Too many questions.

Sucking it up, I chose the place with the least ramifications for my family and headed home. Corrigan's suggestion I buy a gun rang in my head as something to do first thing in the morning. If I lived that long.

I pulled into the apartment's parking spot, kept the motor running and scanned the area. No one about. My hand clutching my can of mace, I raced into the building and up the stairs to my apartment, threw open the door, flicked on the light and looked around. Nothing had been disturbed and nobody was lurking about. I locked and deadbolted the door behind me.

Although exhausted, I felt stinky, like fear had an odor that had settled on me. My shoulders also ached. A hot shower would take care of both the smell and the soreness. I undressed and stepped into the best thing to happen to me all day. For what had to be thirty luxurious minutes, the pulsating water cascaded down me, relaxing me. All good things come to an end and my shower did too. Hating to do so, I turned the water off and stepped onto the bath rug.

While rubbing my skin dry, my ears picked up a noise, and the hairs on my neck stood. After a moment of silence, I decided it was just the furnace readying itself to kick on. It was October, and in Cleveland, that meant one day warm, the next below freezing. In case it wasn't the furnace, I grabbed the only thing I could think of, the toilet bowl brush. Maybe it wouldn't hurt, but it'd definitely gross out any intruder.

First room to check was my bedroom. No one there. I grabbed the mace can from my purse and again checked each room, finding nobody. I collapsed onto the sofa and felt the knot in my stomach loosen. Tomorrow morning and my trip to the gun store couldn't come fast enough.

But the morning did. My phone rang insistently, risking instant death by being thrown across the room. It was 7:00 a.m. A sleepy, yawning, "Hello?"

"Claire? It's Michael. Can I see you this morning?"

He sounded breathless, like he just ran away from someone.

I sat up. "What happened?"

"Can we talk about it in person?"

"Sure. Do you want me to come over?"

"No!" He paused and inhaled deeply. "Your office would be better."

I studied my phone like it had answers to the puzzle of what was going on. "How about at 8:30?"

"Thanks." He ended the call before I could ascertain if he was all right.

I threw on my clothes and gobbled up a cold Pop Tart and water to stop the churning in my stomach. My office wasn't far, but with rush hour traffic it'd take me a while to get there. Flinging a sweater over my shoulder, I headed out, licking the sweetness of the breakfast pastry off my lips.

So preoccupied with Michael's call, I didn't notice something stuck under my windshield wiper until I was already in my car. It was a CD. The parking lot was deserted except for the Romeo who lived in the apartment beneath me and was always with a different woman.

"Excuse me," I shouted. "Did you see anyone around my car this morning?"

He strolled over, looked me up and down, and arched his eyebrow. "No, I didn't." He half smiled. "Or do you want me to say I did?"

I stifled a groan, realizing his assumption I was trying

to strike up a conversation. "No, really. You didn't see anyone?"

Once he understood the message that nobody was hitting on him, he shook his head and returned to his own car.

My first impulse was to grab the CD, but realizing it might have been evidence, used a tissue from my purse to inspect it. Nothing on the label. Had the murderer left it? Had he been lurking around during the night? Would I be keeping that Pop Tart down? Rather than risk removing some evidence by playing the CD, I laid the offensive thing carefully on my car seat and called Corrigan.

From the thickness in his voice, he must have just woken up. "Yeah."

"It's Claire." I tried to keep any hysteria out of my voice. "Someone left an unmarked CD on my windshield."

"Did you see anyone?"

"No, it was here when I came down. There's no label on it or anything."

"Bring it into the station and we'll take a look. Whatever you do, don't play it."

I bit my lip, wanting to scream at him for assuming my stupidity or naivety. But allowing my ego to assert itself wasn't a wise trade for Corrigan's protection. "I'll be there in about twenty minutes."

"Good. And Claire? I'm glad you called me."

"Me too."

In a rush and disconcerted over the CD, I accidentally ran a red light on my way to the station and collected my share of dirty looks and irate horns. Ordinarily, I would sheepishly mouth "Sorry" and truly mean it. But none of my energy could be spared right now. Keeping myself together long enough to turn over the CD was using it up.

Arriving in one piece, I saw Corrigan heading up the steps to go into the station. Without a word, I handed the CD over to him. He slipped it into an evidence bag. "It's a shame you're going through this, but—"

"You don't have to say it. If I had dropped the case in the beginning, none of this would be happening." I sounded like a snotty schoolgirl, but wasn't in the mood for nice. Not now.

He blew out a breath and pointedly finished. "I was going to say, this may help us catch the killer."

I blinked hard. "Huh?" That's me, one snappy comeback after another.

He tilted his head toward the door. "Let's go inside so we can talk."

He motioned to a chair by his desk. "Have a seat. Coffee? Or tea?"

"Neither thanks. What did you mean?" The hairs on my neck stood up and it wasn't because of the station's chilly air.

Corrigan took his time replying. It was obvious to me how much he relished holding my attention, my anticipation of his next words. "Two things." He sipped his coffee. "First, if what I think is on the CD, we'll be able to have our voice experts decipher whether or not the guy is old or young." He stared pointedly at me. "Or if he has an accent, things like that."

I exhaled through clenched teeth. "Or a stutter? Don't you think I'd have noticed things like that?"

He shrugged. "People usually lose their stutter when they sing."

"Okay, but as far as an accent goes, even if I was scared *witless*, I wouldn't have missed that. And you're including Michael in the list of suspects, but he's innocent." *Isn't he?*

Corrigan displayed his straight white teeth in a tolerant smile. "Just saying. It's good for the police to hear it." Before I could respond, he held up two fingers. "Reason number two is that this guy's been to your place. In all likelihood, he'll return, either to up your fears or make good on his threats. But we'll be there to catch him." He sat back in his chair looking like he'd scooped up the last piece of pie.

"You're planning a stakeout at my apartment?"

"Something like that." He templed his fingers. "Haven't worked out all the details yet. But it'll be set before you go home."

I pressed my lips together, not feeling one bit safer. "But what if the guy decides to kill me in some restaurant? Or in the Ladies' room at the hospital while I'm visiting Ed?" Maybe I sounded whiny, but fear did that to me.

"I can't assign a body guard to you, but…" he

swiveled his chair toward me and placed his elbows on his thighs. "It'd be no problem for me to spend a little more time, you know, guarding you."

In another world, I would've tilted my head in a flirty way, pressed my hand against his chest and in a sultry, breathless voice murmured, "You can guard this body anytime."

But we were sitting in a Cleveland police station and someone wanted me eliminated. My tears threatened to burst forth. "Having you watch over me is fine, except for the times you won't be able to. What then?"

He leaned toward me and took my hand, probably hoping I wouldn't start to blubber. "We'll make sure you're never alone." His phone went off and once he'd glanced at it, dropped my hand. "Wait right here." Rising from his chair, he disappeared down a hallway.

He'd been gone about five minutes when I remembered my promise to meet Michael. It was getting late. I tapped my foot, checked the time, and checked it again ten seconds later. Corrigan still hadn't come back so I scribbled a note, apologizing for not waiting. No explanation why. Just a simple note stating he could reach me at my office. No time for another lecture about Michael.

I dashed up the stairs to my office, worried about being tardy for our appointment. Michael was nowhere to be seen. As late as I was, he may have arrived, waited a bit, and left. Hoping he'd come back, I unlocked the office door and locked it behind me. No sense in tempting fate.

I waited ten minutes. Then punched in Michael's number, ready to apologize for not being here. He didn't pick up, though. "It's Claire. Sorry I missed you. Ran into something messy, but I'm at my office now. Call me back, okay?"

My cell rang almost as soon as I'd left the message. It was Corrigan, rather than Michael. "What the hell do you think you're doing? You ask for my help. Then you run out?"

"Sorry. I was late for a meeting." I squeaked.

"With Adler?" he demanded.

"He said he had something to tell me and needed to do it in person." I scrunched up my face, anticipating Corrigan's lecture.

"I bet he does." He heaved a sigh. "You shouldn't be alone with him."

Was he jealous or just wanting to make my life harder? My ego went for jealousy. "It's just a client meeting. All business."

He harrumphed. "Yeah, like last night. I'm on my way there." He ended the call.

Despite my irritation and worry over Michael, I smiled. Two guys had never been interested in me at the same time. That is, except for in third grade when Bucky Minetta and Lenny Schiavone noticed I was really good on the monkey bars.

My thoughts were interrupted by a knock at my door. Corrigan couldn't have gotten here that fast. "Claire, it's

Michael."

Stepping through the doorway, he threw his arms around me. Instinctively, I pulled back and spotted his pained expression. "Michael, what's wrong?"

His face was so contorted he barely resembled the man I'd known. *But how well did I really know him?* Hesitantly, I repeated my question.

He swallowed hard and relaxed his facial muscles. "Corrigan came to see me last night."

A frosty uneasiness settled on me. "And?" It felt like I had swallowed straight pins. Ulcer, anyone?

Michael looked off toward my computer. "Wasn't a social call."

I blew out a breath. "Have a seat." I led him to the chair by my desk. "What exactly did he say?"

Michael sat on the edge. "He thinks I had something to do with my sister's death." He rubbed his face. "I can't believe it. I want them to find her killer too." He stared into my eyes, "You don't think I had anything to do with Constance's death, do you?" His voice soft, pleading.

"Of course not. That's crazy. "It was important to assure him, and myself. "Why does he think that? Did he say?"

Michael shook his head.

"Did he actually accuse you?" My pulse throbbed in my temples. *Did Corrigan have more on Michael than he'd let on?*

He cast his eyes down on the floor and murmured. "Not exactly."

I released a sigh and covered his hand with mine. "Michael, in Detective Corrigan's cynical mind, everyone is a suspect. Don't let him get to you. You already have enough to deal with."

Sitting there in a heavy silence, I couldn't help but wonder if he'd seen Corrigan and me talking last night. Best way to find out was to stick my toe in the water and see if anything bit me. "By the way, when did he visit you?" To my own ears, the strain in my voice made it sound like I'd been the one who committed a crime.

Michael didn't skip a beat. "A bit after you left." He half-smiled. "Glad you weren't around to hear that."

Making a clicking noise like a kid caught with a stolen gumball in my mouth, I nodded. "That means two of us are glad."

"Hate to interrupt all this gladness." It was Corrigan, barging through my office door like a fireman into a burning building.

Chapter Sixteen

There was no misinterpreting the scowl on my face upon realizing I'd left my office door open, allowing every Tom, Dick and Corrigan inside.

Michael jumped to his feet. "I've told you everything."

Corrigan pulled up to his full 6'0" height. "Don't sweat it. This visit is for Miss DeNardo, but as long as you're here, where were you last night after 11:00?"

Michael flinched. "This is unbelievable. Are you accusing me of something else?"

Corrigan's voice turned steely. "Answer the question."

"Home. In bed. Alone." His color rose and he exhaled loudly.

As if it couldn't get worse, my father, with no advanced warning, chose that time to stick his head in.

"Dad?" I sounded like somebody was squeezing my throat.

His eyes moved from Michael to Corrigan and finally

rested on me. "Bad time, Pumpkin?"

Corrigan, in a sweeping motion, answered for me. "Not at all, Mr. DeNardo. Come right in."

I shot the detective a look that cursed him and all his male heirs. "Yeah, it's fine, Dad. What's up?"

My father smiled crookedly. "I wanted to surprise you. Take you to lunch." He glanced at his watch. "It's a little early but I figured, what the heck. You're busy, though." He turned to leave, stopped and swung around. He squinted at Corrigan. "Do I know you?"

I held my breath and hoped Corrigan wouldn't divulge that my father had been under surveillance, courtesy of the Cleveland Police. He didn't blink. "Just figured you were Claire's father. The resemblance is amazing."

My fair skin and dark brown with reddish highlights hair are very different from my dad's olive complexion and black hair now mixed with grey. His Roman nose compared to my upturned one. In short, we look nothing alike. I didn't think for a second my dad bought Corrigan's explanation, but he'd no doubt been taught to be polite to policemen. "Yeah, I guess so." He paused, then squinted at me, "Do you need a hand with anything, honey?"

A quick scan of everyone's face didn't remove my unease. Michael looked down, but not before I spotted his scowl. Corrigan wore an expression like a choirboy with a slingshot in his back pocket. And my dad looked eager to help me, even if he wasn't sure how.

There was a way, though. Break up the trio of Corrigan, Michael and me by leaving with my dad. Afterwards, I'd regroup with Michael to talk with him alone, and check in with Corrigan later about protection. "Dad, if you'll give me just a few minutes, it'd be great to have lunch with you." My grin could compete with any smile a clown chose to paint on. I was proud of my plan until Corrigan pasted his own on top of mine.

The wily detective rubbed his chin. "Hey, why don't we all go to lunch?" Before anyone could protest he added, "I'll even drive."

No one said a word, but that didn't deter his faux-enthusiasm. "This'll be great. Adler, you can ride in the front with me. Claire and Mr. DeNardo, in the backseat." When no one moved, Corrigan took my arm as if he were my prom escort.

I pulled away and Michael finally found his voice. He stuck his hand out to my dad. "Sir, I'm Michael Adler. It's a pleasure to meet you, but I have to excuse myself from this outing." He threw a look toward Corrigan as if he hoped the man would be mowed down by a runaway elephant.

My father stood there, dumbfounded at all of this, but he shook Michael's hand anyway. "Good to meet you too, Mr. Adler." Dad looked at me like he did when I came home past curfew. I had some explaining to do.

Corrigan grinned widely and in a master-of-ceremonies voice said, "Too bad, Adler. I'm sure we could've had a great conversation over lunch." He jangled his car keys. "Well, Mr. DeNardo, Claire, let's get going before the crowds get there. Adler, why don't you lead the way out?"

Michael's nostrils flared and he gave me a why-don't-you-do-something look. Almost outside my office, he leaned toward me and whispered, "I'll call you later."

Once again Corrigan took my arm and led me through the door with my father following. His act was beyond belief.

Dad sat in the front seat with Corrigan at my insistence. This way, I could seethe in the back. Once we'd eaten and my father left, the brash detective would get a piece of my mind. Not that there were many pieces left, but wasn't this a form of police harassment?

We ended up at The Citrus Tree, a cute bistro that managed to garner awards every year. It was a shame I wouldn't enjoy the food, being too occupied, waiting for my opportunity to stab Corrigan with my fork. With my knife if he said anything to make my dad suspicious. Like Dad wouldn't already be.

When Corrigan made some menu recommendations, my eyebrows rose. He didn't seem like the bistro type. More like hole-in-the-wall Chinese takeout.

"Do you come here often?" Those words made me grimace. Put together, they sounded like a trite pickup line.

Corrigan closed his menu and gave me a lazy smile. "Enough to know what's good."

My father sat bullet straight, obviously ill at ease.

"Claire, honey, maybe this was a mistake coming here. I can't pick anything. The cavatelli with meat sauce sounds good, but no one could make it like your mother. That woman spoiled me, you know." He looked down at the table, but it was plain to see her memory cracked through my dad's veneer.

I grabbed his hand under the table and gave it a squeeze. "She was a great cook."

"And a beautiful woman." He smiled and squeezed my hand back.

Hard to believe, but Corrigan had this sentimental expression on his face like he'd soon be dewy-eyed and mushy. I didn't take him for a softie, but maybe he was human beneath that gorgeous exterior and cop steel.

Corrigan's voice was quiet and full of compassion. "I'm sorry for your loss. How long has your wife been gone?"

My father absently twisted his wedding band. "Too long."

I leaned in. "A little over three years."

"My father passed on about six years ago. My mother still misses him."

Dad nodded. "Sometimes it's hard to go on when one of your biggest reasons is gone." He added quickly, "Course, I have my Claire." He smiled warmly at me. "Don't know what I'd do without her."

I grinned. "And Aunt Lena."

He looked to the ceiling. "Yeah, she'd kill me if I died before her."

We all laughed and the tension between my shoulders dissipated. At least until my phone vibrated. Twice. Both calls were from Michael.

By the time we returned to the office it was as if my dad and Corrigan had known each other forever. Corrigan was never more charming, at least not around me. It seemed genuine. The two men clicked, even so far as telling each other Italian and Irish jokes.

But after my father left, first kissing me and thanking Corrigan over and over for a great time, my shoulders rose again. I could feel the throb of yet another impending headache.

"Your father's a great guy. It was a real pleasure to meet him."

"Yes, he is. Thank you for not saying anything about the case. But why in the world take us—"

"I became your bodyguard the minute I stepped into your office. Until we catch the killer, you won't be alone with anyone."

I raised an eyebrow. "Not just Michael?"

"Anyone." He half-smiled. "Except maybe your father."

"How can you watch me twenty-four hours a day?" I smirked. "Or don't you need sleep?"

"Don't worry about me. All the arrangements have been made."

"What does that mean?"

He stuck his hands in his pockets. "It'll be me, Officer Dobrowski, or Officer Washington. Both good cops."

"Guess that will work for me. But I have someone to meet later…"

"Adler. Go ahead." He closed the space between us, cupped my chin with his hand, and in a husky whisper said, "Remember, I won't be far away."

My heart slapped a high-five with my lungs, and I was breathless and dizzy at the same time. Why did he come into my life just when I might be murdered? "I won't forget."

He stepped back and gave a curt nod. "Good. Now where to?"

"To see Ed. He's first." But the vibration of my phone told me otherwise. Michael, again. I rubbed my face and, this time, took his call.

"Claire, it's Michael. We need to finish our talk."

With the detective close by, I didn't want to reveal the caller or anything about this conversation. "We will. Promise."

"Good. Can we make it tonight?"

Corrigan was busy checking his messages. "Of course."

"Corrigan's listening, isn't he?"

My eyes shifted to Corrigan. "Good guess."

"Let's meet at my house. 6:00 tonight. I can make dinner."

Although my taste buds pleaded with me for another Michael-made meal, I preferred someplace more public. "How about the Shellfish Shanty? On West 130th?"

Corrigan's ears perked up like a hound dog hunting squirrel.

"Why not here? I'll make scallops with linguini. Strawberries Romanoff for dessert."

When a shiver rolled down my spine, I was unsure as to whether it was an anticipated food orgasm or because he sounded like a spider inviting a fly to dinner. The latter seemed ridiculous and so I dismissed it from my mind. Still, with my tone as sweet as frosting on a cinnamon bun, I turned his offer down. "Sounds wonderful, but the Shanty has been on my list of restaurants to go to for a long time."

Suspicion gave an edge to his voice. "Claire, is something bothering you? Has Corrigan been hitting on you? Be careful with him. He's more interested in you than in solving Constance's murder." He sounded like I'd crushed his heart.

I cradled my chin. *Don't trust Michael. Don't trust Corrigan.* It seemed the only person trustworthy was my father. Okay, and Aunt Lena.

"Nothing's wrong." A wave of sympathy for him hit me, and I would have agreed to meet him at his house, but that idea of the spider kept weaving itself into my thoughts. "We can finish our talk at the Shellfish Shanty. At six, it's so dead." I crinkled my face at that last comment.

Michael sighed. "Okay. If that's what you want."

I smiled, relieved. Corrigan hadn't created a disturbance between Michael and me despite his best efforts.

Corrigan watched me pull my car keys from my pocket. “Put your keys away. I’m driving you.”

“I’m not supposed to drive myself?”

He ignored my sarcasm. “No sense in taking two cars. I wanted to check in on Ed myself.” When I didn’t put my keys away, he added, “I’ll bring you back here afterwards.”

My keys went back into my pocket, and we returned to his car. He pulled out of the lot, stared straight ahead, and murmured, “After the hospital, we’ll swing by the station. See if the audio people have anything.” He turned casually to me and added, “Then I’ll drop you off. You can go home and freshen up. Just remember, I’ll be around in case he gets too fresh.”

I looked up and sighed. “It’s not a date.”

He chuckled, like he was really enjoying this. “Of course not. But your safety is my concern.”

I gritted my teeth. “You sound like a safety technician.”

He let loose with a hardy laugh. “You’re right about that. But seriously, I don’t want anything bad happening to you.” His voice softened. “I’d never forgive myself.”

My insides turned all marshmallowy. It felt good to have someone watch over me, since this case scared me beyond words.

I touched his forearm. “I’ll try not to make your job harder than it is.”

His lopsided grin appeared. “Does that mean you’ll

cancel with Adler?"

I pulled my hand back. "No, it doesn't."

Less than five minutes later, we arrived at the hospital. Corrigan spoke with the uniformed cop who still guarded Ed, and then with Ed's nurse. There'd been no change. Corrigan accompanied me into Ed's room.

"Would you mind me being alone with him for a little bit? I promise not to go anywhere without you."

Corrigan nodded. "If you need me, tell the guard. I'm going to talk with Ed's doc and then come back."

Left alone with Ed, it seemed natural to pull a chair close to his bed, and wrap his hand in mine. I sat motionless, trying to send him…I don't know…some good energy. The noise of all the equipment faded into the background. Hoping he'd miraculously grab onto mine, I removed my hand. Nothing happened. My eyes moistened and guilt shrouded me.

The guard stuck his head inside the door. "Miss, since you're here, mind if I take a, you know, break? It's right down the hall."

"No problem. Do what you need to do." He thanked me and his footsteps faded down the corridor.

I watched Ed's breathing. In and out, until my breaths matched his. If only it was within my power to wake him up. But no amount of staring helped.

I checked the time. Eight minutes since the guard had left.

After fifteen minutes, I poked my head out the door and scanned the hallway. No guard and no Corrigan. A ball of tension formed in my stomach. Swallowing hard was the only way to keep it from migrating to my throat. I sat down and popped right back up. Something was wrong.

My call went straight to Corrigan's voicemail. I decided to get someone to go into the men's room, took two steps outside, and glanced up and down the hall.

Four males dressed in street clothes and some hospital staff along with carts and poles filled the corridor. One man in particular caught my attention. He was headed down the hall, away from me. From the back, he looked like Michael. But what would Michael be doing here?

Although I wanted to run after this could-be Michael, Ed couldn't be left unguarded. The next best thing would have to do. "Michael!"

A twenty-something guy with dark hair turned around and came toward me to see who had called the name out and why. But the man who resembled Michael never hesitated. Instead, he kept walking and disappeared around a corner.

After apologizing to the young man who I had stopped by mistake, I texted Corrigan.

This time he called me. "Problem?"

"Ed's guard has been gone for almost twenty minutes."

Corrigan didn't scoff at me for worrying over nothing. "Be right there. Don't move." He showed up so fast he must have used a gurney and skateboarded in.

"First, Ed's okay?"

"Yes. The guard said he needed the restroom. Please go look for him."

"Be right back." He dashed off.

My concern for Ed battled against my curiosity. The next person in a hospital uniform who walked by got yanked into Ed's room. I dug out my identification and flew it past her. "Police business. Stay with this patient until notified otherwise."

She scowled but gave me a curt nod.

I ran to the men's room, but stopped outside the door and put my ear against it. I probably looked like a pervert who hoped to sneak a peek at some willies.

From inside, Corrigan called the guard's name while someone, probably the guard, moaned.

Something had to be done. I pushed the door open and rushed in. Blood dripped from the back of the guard's head as he lay cradled in Corrigan's arms. When Corrigan saw me, he yelled, "Get a doctor. Now."

I galloped through the hallway like Paul Revere. "Doctor! I need a doctor!"

A heavyset nurse marched over to me. "What's the problem?"

"A man's bleeding." I pointed toward the restroom. "Hurry."

We speed-walked into the men's room and knelt down. After a quick inspection of the guard, the nurse declared, "He'll need sutures." She heaved herself up. "Let's get him into a wheelchair and then down to

Emergency."

After the nurse left to find that wheelchair, the guard tried to stand, but Corrigan gently held him down."Easy, Walters. We'll get you up when the nurse comes back. Now, what happened?"

Walters's eyes rolled upwards and for a second it looked like he'd pass out again. His eyelids fluttered open and he focused his eyes. "Not sure. I was taking a whiz, pardon, using the john, when someone came behind me. Cold cocked me."

"Did you see anything?" Corrigan asked.

"Nah. Not a good idea to check out other guys when you're in here."

The nurse returned with an aide pushing a wheelchair. "Mark will take you to the ER." Corrigan and Mark loaded the injured cop into the chair.

Corrigan patted the guard's shoulder. "I'll check on you in a minute."

We followed them out and Corrigan hurried me back to Ed's room. The woman I'd drafted to watch Ed stood next to the door, arms crossed, tapping her foot. In return for my thanks, she merely harrumphed.

"Pleasant woman," Corrigan remarked. He made a call and when it was over, explained, "Someone to replace Walters will be here in thirty minutes. We stay put until then."

The wait seemed longer than half an hour. Corrigan, hands twisted behind his back, paced rapidly as we waited. Either the floor or his shoes would soon wear out.

I returned to the chair beside Ed, mesmerized by the pattern on his heart monitor. Sort of made a game of it, promising myself the next time it spiked up, I'd tell Corrigan that Michael might be here. True to my promise, I began, "While I was waiting for Ed's guard, I might have—"

Heavy footsteps interrupted my confession. Corrigan's attention was directed at the replacement. "It's about damn time." Lowering his voice, he briefed the new guy. Then he motioned to me. "Come on. Let's see if Walters is okay and if he remembers anything else."

The last stroke I saw on the monitor was a downward one. But I disregarded it and, as we got closer to the ER, I cleared my throat. "While you were in with Walters, I might have seen Michael."

Corrigan came to a dead stop. "What do mean *might* have?"

I half-shrugged. "From the back, it looked like Michael. But when I called to him, the guy didn't turn around or even hesitate. And there was no way he didn't hear me."

"Was this guy coming from the men's room or going in there?" His voice terse.

"Neither. He was just walking down the hall."

Corrigan huffed, pulled out the notepad he always carried and wrote something down. He stuck it back in his jacket and mumbled, "Maybe now you're not so convinced Adler is innocent in all this."

I didn't reply. I didn't want Corrigan to be right that Michael shouldn't be trusted. Besides being my client, my feelings for him were…more than businesslike. Maybe the guy I saw wasn't Michael. Or was I just blinded by the fact that the man could cook and bake like Betty Crocker and Duncan Hines mixed together?

Down in the ER, Officer Walters lay on a gurney, a bulky bandage around his head. He was more alert now, but didn't have anything new to add, even when Corrigan asked him if he'd noticed a tall, balding, thirtyish man with thick glasses. I relaxed a bit when Walters didn't recall any such person. When we were done, Corrigan ushered me outside the room and the hospital.

Once we reached the visitor's parking lot, I glanced around for Michael's car. Corrigan pulled out his keys. "Not that it means anything, but if you're looking for Adler's car, I've already checked and it isn't here."

That was a relief.

Corrigan backed his car out of his parking space. Without looking at me he said, "They checked for prints on that CD. The only ones on it are yours."

"Not a surprise." But I wished there had been fingerprints all over the CD belonging to Eagleton. "Has anyone asked Eagleton or his trusty sidekick where they were last night?"

"I'm on it. Don't worry."

Me, not worry? The cowardly part of me, a big part, wanted to let Corrigan handle it. But I couldn't just sit by and be killed waiting for him to do something. My decision to visit Eagleton after a quick dinner with Michael was more about survival than bravery.

In that weird way one thought leads to another, that one brought me back to wondering if it had been Michael at the hospital. If so, why didn't he respond to my call? Could he possibly have anything to do with Walters being attacked? I chewed on my lower lip, hashing it out. My instinct told me he did. Damn my instinct.

We waited for a red light to change. His eyes on the road, Corrigan said, "Audio team gave me their report too. Another song from *West Side Story*. Couldn't do much with the voice. It was altered." The light turned green and we cruised through. "But we'll still need you to hear it."

I'd rather go to the dentist and have all my teeth drilled, than listen. But what other choice was there?

A look at the time told me I'd probably have to go straight from my office to dinner. At least it would be at the Shanty rather than at Michael's house. This way, I could ask my questions about seeing him at the hospital in public.

***

My behind was turning numb waiting in the uncomfortable chair by Corrigan's desk. He was hunting down the report on the CD. When I'd given up hope for blood ever returning to my posterior, he showed up, running his fingers through his hair as he scanned the report. He frowned and tossed it on his desk. "Nothing here I haven't already told you."

"Figured as much." I stood up. "You still need me to listen to it?" Eating fried spiders sounded more appealing.

"Yep. And they should be ready for us."

He led me to a small room full of black and silver gadgets with lots of knobs and switches. Motioning for me to sit, he introduced me to Henry, the technician, and someone else whose name I didn't catch.

Henry pushed his glasses up and smiled at me. "Ready?"

Corrigan leaned over so his face was close to mine, and he placed his hands on the arms of my chair. "Take your time. We can replay it if you need."

Yeah, why don't we play it so much I go home humming it?

My legs wiggled and my resolve melted like a popsicle dropped on a hot sidewalk. Still, I said, "I'm ready."

At first I heard a high pitched buzz on the CD. The voice sang to the tune of "Gee, Officer Krupke" and almost blotted out the noise.

"Dear stupid little piggy,

I warned you off this case.

Now I'm gonna kill you.

It seems like such a waste.

It's not that I don't like you,

It's business don't you know,

Gee little piggy, you gotta go."

The song ended and Henry shut it off, but that buzz in my ears continued, traveling into my brain and spinning around, making me dizzy and nauseated. I felt hot all over.

Corrigan's hand was on my back then, handing me a cup of water. I took a sip. Better now, maybe because of the water. Or Corrigan, with his eyes full of concern. I took in a shaky breath and blew it out. "I'm okay now."

"Sorry to put you through that. Did you recognize anything?"

"Not really." I took another sip of water. "Could you play it again?" I hoped to not throw up.

I listened again to the whole, sick thing. It wasn't any easier the second time. But the background noise was familiar. "I know what that noise is."

Henry and I became a duo when we both pronounced, "It's a circular saw." I went on. "But that isn't very significant. All my uncles, my neighbors, even my dad have one."

Corrigan thanked the audio team and ushered me out of the room. He rubbed his neck. "I'll take you back to your office. Get your car, and I'll follow you to the Shellfish Shanty."

My mind's eye saw it all unfold. Corrigan asking for a cozy table for three: him, Michael and me.

We pulled up to my car and before I got out, he said, "Act natural at the restaurant."

Act natural? I'm naturally terrified. Out of the corner of my mouth I asked, "Will you be at a nearby table, spying on us over the menu?"

He snorted. "Give me more credit than that. This isn't my first time." He added almost under his breath, "First time I had a personal interest, though."

I rewarded him with a smile fit for a homecoming queen, but didn't say anything, afraid I'd spoil it. I brushed his cheek with my fingertips and he turned toward me. Our eyes met, but before any violins could play Rachmaninoff, another driver, some guy in a fancy car, laid on his horn. "You're blocking the driveway. Move it."

So much for any hubba-hubba, as my dad would say. Corrigan nodded toward the 'Do Not Block Driveway' sign and cursed under his breath. He jerked the car forward enough for the outraged driver to get by.

Chapter Seventeen

After a few last-minute instructions from Corrigan, I drove to the Shellfish Shanty. My stomach churned but it wasn't from hunger. Every few seconds, my eyes studied my rearview mirror. Corrigan was right where he told me he'd be. I used the restaurant's valet parking. No dark deserted side streets for me. Corrigan had parked himself, but I took it on faith he could keep me in his sights.

I tossed my hair back in an attempt to throw off any fear. It wasn't as if I'd never been with Michael alone before. No big deal.

My entrance into the restaurant was memorable since I jerked like a marionette in the hands of a new apprentice. Michael waved and stood up. The perfect gentleman. Scanning the room didn't provide me with a Corrigan sighting. Still, I stuck a smile on my face and greeted Michael like nothing had changed. My mouth felt prickly, as if it were full of straw.

He took my offered hand and guided me to my chair.

Then he bent toward me, going for a quick kiss, but I wasn't interested and turned my head so his lips brushed my hair instead. Too bad I hadn't shampooed. He waited for me to sit, then followed suit.

Before I could choke on a fib like, 'Good to see you,' the waitress hurried over and asked for our drink order.

"Just water for me, thanks." I'd need all my wits about me to find out if he was at the hospital today and if so, why he ignored me.

Michael cocked his head. "Are you sure?" He leaned in and whispered like a co-conspirator. "Let's both get a chocolate cherry martini."

Ordinarily, the thought of chocolate liqueur, cherry vodka, chocolate syrup, and a cherry on top makes me swoon, but I couldn't chance it. Still, my conditioned response was to drool like a Saint Bernard. "Can't, Michael. But you go ahead."

He shook his head and just ordered water too. "No fun drinking one of those alone." He placed his hand over mine and his eyes twinkled. "But it seems like we've both had a tough day and we do deserve a drink."

There was my opening. "Oh? What did you do today?"

He straightened his placemat. "Errands. Mostly downtown. Should've taken the Rapid, but I drove." He took a sip of his water and wiped his mouth. "Traffic was awful. Wasn't even sure I'd make it here on time." He paused. "So what about that drink?"

I held up my hand to decline again, wanting to get

back to the questioning. But unwinding a bit did sound good. I would let my chocolate-loving soul delight in one relaxing drink before putting Michael back under my exam light. I'd have to be careful, though, or risk accusing him of God-knows-what.

We made small talk until our drinks came. I took a couple sips of the glorious concoction and it fortified me. I'd play it cool. But that phrase reminded me of the West Side Story song, *Cool,* "Just play it cool boy, Real cool", bringing back the horror of those threatening calls. I took a shaky breath and willed my face into a fake calm. Placid, like a riverboat gambler holding a straight flush. Making sure I could once again speak in a pitch lower than a referee's whistle, I asked, "Did any of those errands take you to Fairview Hospital?"

He shook his head. "No. Why do you ask?"

My eyes remained on my martini glass. "I thought I saw you and wondered what you were doing there."

"It wasn't me."

A sip of water instead of my drink was wise. Putting the glass down, I spoke as if to myself. "Funny. The guy sure looked like you."

A vein in his forehead throbbed. "You don't believe me?" He swirled the liquid in his glass.

I dropped my hands in my lap and clasped them together to stop from fidgeting. "No, just wondered. Guess I made a mistake." If that line was any more transparent I could hang curtains around it. My mouth went dry. "Sorry Michael. But I *am* a private investigator. It's my job to be curious, and that means being curious about someone who looked a lot like you being at the hospital and ignoring me, like he had something to hide."

The stakes in this what-are-you-up-to game were too high for me to play coy. I ran my finger through the condensation on my martini glass and wondered if he'd seen me with Corrigan and Ed's guard.

He looked me directly in the eyes. "Understood." A hint of a smile. "I know you have to ask questions, but please don't be like Corrigan."

"Huh?"

"Suspicious of everything I do."

My stomach did a roller coaster dive. That was exactly what I was doing, and needed to. He still hadn't doused that flame of doubt burning in me. But I couldn't grab him by the collar and make him talk so I used the tools God gave me; dazzled him with my sugar-substitute sweet smile. "Not to worry. Still, why—"

He laid his hands palm down on the table, his voice firm. "I wasn't there." He waited a heartbeat, then, "But what were you doing at the hospital?"

I'd prepared for him asking, and the fib rolled off my tongue. "A friend of my father's was admitted, and my dad asked me to visit him. He was asleep when I got there, though." I downed some water to shut myself up. When I'm not telling the truth my tendency is to expand unnecessarily on the lie. If I didn't watch it, I'd explain the diagnosis, treatment and prognosis of this imaginary friend. Then cap it off by talking about the folks he'd leave behind.

Michael finished his drink. "You'll go back again then?" Without asking me, he ordered two more drinks.

I covered my martini glass with my hand. "One's plenty for me. And yes, I'll go back to see him again."

He picked up my hand. "Please. One more."

Not a good idea, especially on an empty stomach. "I really can't."

Any further debate over another drink was postponed by my phone's jingling. A text message from Corrigan. I excused myself. "Have to take care of this. Be back in a second."

"Of course." Michael stood as I left the table.

I ducked into the restroom. Corrigan's message explained he'd been called away, but my second-shift body guard would arrive shortly. In caps he added, "STAY PUT!!!" So much for 24 hour protection. My deodorant's promise was more reliable.

I splashed cold water on my face to revive my brain and headed back to the table, expecting Michael to resume his questioning. It was vital that I be ready for him. What I hadn't prepared for, though, was the second round of drinks he'd ordered.

Having no choice but to ignore the drink by my dinner setting, I apologized for the interruption.He waved his hand, as if the subject now totally bored him. "It's certainly all right." He smiled but his eyes didn't reflect happy times. He picked up his menu. "What looks good?"

At this point anything would relieve my drink's effect. The room wasn't exactly spinning. More like it was a big ship on a choppy sea. I hoped my alcohol-doused stomach wouldn't reject the food and force any morsels to make a second less-than-savory appearance.

A little voice inside kept poking me, urging me to ask more questions. Another voice told that first one to shut up and enjoy the dinner. The first voice won. "You were pretty upset with Corrigan this afternoon. Now it seems you've dismissed it. Why? What's happened?"

He lowered his menu. His face turned partly cloudy. Then the sun came out. "I decided to rise above it. After all, I haven't really done anything wrong," he lowered his eyes, "except maybe like my private detective too much."

I forced a smile. My feelings for him had faded like a cheap hair dye. "We should order dinner."

Instead of calling the waitress over, though, he raised his drink. "A toast. To Claire for dropping the case."

I picked up my water glass instead my martini and took a short gulp.

Michael suppressed a smile. "Rather have water, huh? Glad I asked for refills." He took a small sip of his drink, and watched me over his glass.

We finally ordered and he raised his drink again. "A second toast. To a happy friendship that may become more."

All of a sudden, I got very thirsty, and lifting my

water glass, drained it. Then wiped my mouth with the back of my hand like I just drank from a garden hose. My attempts to rest my chin on my hand were futile; it kept slipping off. The room seemed overly warm, and I undid the top button of my blouse.

"Claire, are you all right?"

I blinked hard to get his two heads back into one. At this rate, eating off the floor would be my only choice because that's where I'd be laying. My body swayed in the chair. "I'm fine."

I was anything but.

Michael spoke but I didn't hear him. Instead, my head buzzed. The last thing I remember was imagining Michael as a fat bumble bee.

Chapter Eighteen

It was still dark when I woke up in Michael's guestroom. My head felt like someone had dropped an anvil on it, and my mouth seemed full of fuzz. I frantically patted myself to make sure my clothes were still on. They were twisted and wrinkled, but everything was in place, except for my shoes. They were next to the bed.

Using the bedside table, I steadied myself and slipped my shoes on. Michael must have hauled me out of the restaurant before my second-shift bodyguard came. Was that a coincidence or had he cunningly figured out how to separate me from my safety net? If so, why? Visions of Ed at the bottom of my office stairs. Or, of Mallorie, lifeless at my door, compounded my fears. No harm had come to me—yet. I wrapped my arms around myself.

Corrigan must be frantic.

Calling him was impossible. My phone was no longer in my pocket. Not that telling Corrigan where I'd spent the night would be pleasant. But without my phone, it wasn't an option. Panic began behind my eyes and the feeling spread to my stomach. Not satisfied to stay there, it coursed down my legs giving them the strength of gummy worms.

"Claire?" Michael knocked, interrupting my paranoia.

"Don't come in. I, I'm not dressed." My eyes darted around the room, searching for my purse. It lay open on top of a chair across the room and I groped around inside it. Although my phone was gone, he hadn't taken my mace. The spray canister slipped out of my grasp once, but when I managed to pull it out of my purse, I tiptoed close to the door and took aim. "Come in." With no idea what harm he meant to me, my index finger sat poised on the spray button.

Michael walked in holding a tray with soup, bread, a cup of tea, and a pink carnation in a vase. His smile vanished when he saw the mace. "What are you doing?"

My eyes never left him. "Why did you drug me?" *Great ice breaker.*

The tray slanted and the glass vase knocked against the tea cup, creating a tinkling sound. "What are you talking about? How could you even think such a thing?"

I removed my finger from the button but held the mace tight, now unsure whether to feel guilty for accusing him like that or to be even more suspicious. Better to be wary than sorry. "Did you?"

Someone pounded on his front door before he got the chance to either defend himself or confess.

"Police. Open up."

Michael's hands tightened on the tray. Through clenched teeth he asked, "Did you call the police?"

"How could I? My phone's gone. You should know that; you took it." I pushed past him and fiddled with the door lock, trying to open it. I called through the door. "I'm here, just a—"

Michael, having dropped the tray on the hallway table, pulled me away from the door and with one quick turn, unlocked and opened it.

Corrigan and another cop I assumed was his partner appeared ready to pounce.

Michael, feet apart and fists clenched by his side, demanded, "Why are you here?"

"May we come in?" Without waiting for Michael's response, Corrigan muscled past him. The detective's eyes took in my disheveled condition and the tray. He cleared his throat and out of the corner of his mouth said, "Sure hope we weren't interrupting your bedtime snack."

"What? No. It's not what you think." My relief at seeing Corrigan morphed into outrage.

He looked up toward the ceiling. "Gather up your things, little lady, you need to come with us right now."

Little lady? Were we in the Old West? I'd correct him later on. The current priority was to get away from Michael.

Michael frowned and placed his hand lightly on my arm. "Why does she have to go?"

Corrigan's voice took on a confidential tone. "She's

wanted for questioning."

I pulled away from Michael, and in a strong-woman voice said, "Come on. You came here looking for me and here I am. Let me grab my purse and we can go." A dozen more questions hung in the air, waiting for Michael's explanations, but my desire to get away from him was stronger than my curiosity about being drugged.

We were inside the car, me in the backseat, Corrigan and his partner in the front. I leaned as far forward as my seatbelt would let me. "How did you know where to come get me?"

I could see the scowl on Corrigan's face as he showed me my cell phone. "Found it in the Ladies' room at the Shanty."

"So that's where it was." I grabbed for the phone, hoping Corrigan wouldn't ask and I wouldn't tell him about being 'under the influence.' "That still doesn't explain how—"

"Didn't take detective work. You were last seen with Adler. Unbeknownst to your protection, you left the restaurant. That led to my conclusion you had gone somewhere with Adler, probably his home."

We stopped at a light and he spun around, straining against his seatbelt. His voice was a low rumble. "That was a dumb stunt. You were lucky we found you before anything happened." His neck muscles bulged.

"Like what? He'd soil my good name?" I crossed my arms. "I could've gotten out of there without your interference."

He snorted and hit the gas hard. “Yeah. How? By blinding him with the tea? Or knocking him unconscious with the carnation?”

My head ached and my tongue felt like it needed a shave. “I would’ve found a way. And what have you done with my car?” *That’s right, put him on the offensive.*

For the first time, the other detective spoke. “It’s at the station.”

“Thank *you.*” I emphasized the ‘you.’ Sure, that was as childish as sticking my tongue out at Corrigan, but who cared. “And just so you know, going to Michael’s wasn’t my idea. I was drugged.”

Corrigan gave a short, harsh laugh. “I’ve heard that one before.”

I wanted to smash my purse into his face. “It’s true. In fact, I want a take a blood test to prove it.”

His seen-it-all look evaporated. “Did that bastard hurt you?”

“No. But if you hadn’t come when you did…” I couldn’t finish the thought.

Corrigan released a breath. “You can get the test done at the station.”

I steeled myself for Corrigan’s next comment. When it didn’t come, I closed my eyes.

By the time my eyes opened again, we’d arrived at the police station. Corrigan parked the car. “So you know, the Adler case has moved forward.”

After donating a vial of blood to prove I’d been

drugged, I found my way to Corrigan's desk. He handed me a cup of coffee. "Sorry it's not on a silver tray."

"Very funny." I took the cup. Maybe the bitter, hot brew would help get rid of the drumming in my head. "How has the case progressed?"

"Brought Eagleton in. He should be ready for questioning," he glanced at his watch, "Right about now."

"Are you charging him with murder? Why now?"

He pulled a chair out. "Have a seat."

Once I sat down he followed suit. "Eagleton was always in our sights, but we didn't have enough on him until now."

"What changed?" Curiosity mingled with relief that the evidence pointed to Brody Eagleton.

Corrigan paused and caught his lower lip between his teeth as if deciding whether to play his whole hand. He leaned forward. "The soon-to-be-former Mrs. Eagleton."

"His wife?" My eyes narrowed. "That's who you left me for last night?" My face turned red, as it dawned on me I sounded like a jealous lover. "I mean what..."

Amusement danced across his face but quickly disappeared. "She found a letter from her husband to Constance, and insisted on only talking to me. The letter was a threatening one, like the ones Adler showed us. We believe Eagleton sent Constance those letters and then followed through with the threats. Incidentally, we're going to need those letters from Adler. It's unclear how they slipped away."

I flinched like he'd thrown those letters at me, remembering all too clearly advising Michael to keep quiet about them.

Oblivious to my potential anxiety attack, Corrigan leaned back in his chair, hands clasped behind his head. "We were able to ascertain the suspect owns a circular saw, and we know he's a fan of *West Side Story*."

"Sounds like you have it all wrapped up. Why do you need me?"

"If he's charged with murder we want you to press assault charges against him for sending you those threatening messages. He's been a busy boy."

"Press assault charges? Isn't that sort of overkill?" My faux pas slipped past Corrigan. He didn't skip a beat.

"We want to make sure he gets all that's coming to him. He has an alibi for Mallorie's murder, but not for Ed's assault." Another detective motioned to Corrigan, and he rose. "Make yourself comfortable, Claire. This could take a while."

Instead of 'a while,' Corrigan should have warned me it would take until infinity. After fifteen minutes of sitting, I paced for a while. Sat down again and closed my eyes. When my head flopped down on my chest, my eyes popped open. I went in search of coffee and wandered into the break room, where I must have dozed off again. My coffee had turned cold. Corrigan had to have returned by now.

Before going back to his desk, I ducked into the ladies room and stood in front of the sink, washing my hands and looking into the mirror. One side of my face was red and lined like it'd been pressed against my arm.

My mind reviewed everything that had happened, starting with when Michael first walked into my office. I'd been sure in the beginning Eagleton had killed Constance, but now my doubts prevented me from celebrating his arrest.

I picked at a fingernail. How did Eagleton get hold of a letter Michael claims he wrote? I wanted to tell Corrigan about that, but I'd get into trouble for sure. That was withholding evidence, even if my intentions were innocent. A chill ran down my spine. Prison orange wouldn't compliment my skin at all. My father's heart would break like eggs. Who'd be there to help Aunt Lena at *Cannoli's*? No, it wouldn't do for me to tell Corrigan the truth flat out. Maybe a well-placed hint would do it.

Corrigan was already at his desk, tie loosened, hint of a pale beard, and his hair ruffled, typing furiously. He looked up. "Have a good nap?" He seemed exhausted, but satisfied. "Well, we got him. Case looks good for Eagleton murdering Constance and for the attempt on Ed. His alibi for Mallorie's may not withstand close inspection, either."

"Are you sure you've got the right guy?" My high-pitched voice betrayed all the tension I was feeling.

Corrigan's eyebrow shot up. "You kept saying from the start it was Eagleton. Don't tell me you're having second thoughts."

I hated Debate in school. If I was ahead,

overwhelming sympathy for my opponent forced me to lose the argument on purpose, a habit I had to break. "It's just that…what if Constance gave the threatening letter to Eagleton and he kept it? And, you said yourself lots of people like *West Side Story*. And practically everyone has a circular saw." I took a deep breath. "What about my being drugged? How does that fit into Eagleton as the killer?"

Corrigan stared at me and tapped his fingers on his desk. After what seemed to be five minutes but was probably five seconds, he resumed typing, pounding hard on each key.

I cleared my throat as if to say, "I'm still here."

"When your test results come back, I'll personally question Adler. God knows what sick thing he may have had in mind. In the meantime, stay away from him. Finish any business with him electronically. You're too…" He stopped and looked like he wanted to swallow his tongue.

"Too what? Short? Stupid? Undeniably gorgeous?"

"Nothing. And, as for the rest, we've got the right guy." He paused then added, "Do you want to press assault charges against Eagleton now?"

"Not yet. Some family issues need handling right now." I maintained an air of cooperation I sure didn't feel. "As soon as possible, though."

Corrigan sprang up. "Claire, I know you disagree with charging Eagleton, but don't go digging on your own. Whether you believe it or not, it could still be dangerous."

I managed a distracted smile. "Understood. But family business won't wait. Be back before…before the rooster crows twice." *Really?* I dashed off before he could ask me what the hell that meant.

I signed some police paperwork to get my car back. If Corrigan didn't believe Michael had anything to do with Constance's death, I'd have to get the evidence myself. My fingers shook trying to get the key in the ignition. There was a movie once where a goat was used as bait. I was that goat.

Chapter Nineteen

Most people when faced with unpleasantness or danger lose their appetite. On the other hand, my cravings for the most decadent foodstuffs begin just before I head into the mouth of possible destruction. Maybe my body hoped, in the case of my demise, to least have a recent, final and delightful memory.

I stopped at Breadsmith's Café to get some iced tea and a chocolate banana muffin handsomely drizzled with more chocolate.

Munching away, the quietness of the café struck me. A smart place to meet with Michael and ask him some questions. Other customers sat at tables so we wouldn't be alone. I just needed to make sure he didn't have any opportunity to put anything in my food or drink.

I pulled out my phone and frowned. The battery was dead and my charger was at home. I chugged the tea and walked out chewing the muffin, probably leaving a trail of crumbs of which Hansel and Gretel would approve.

It would only take me a few minutes to get from my

office back to the café. I could make the call to Michael from my office land line.

He picked up on the first ring like he'd been waiting for my call.

"Michael, it's Claire. Sorry about earlier. Just my morning paranoia getting the best of me. Please accept my apologies." When necessary, I could be a talented groveler.

"You're forgiven. Now what did Corrigan ask you about?"

"I'll tell you everything in person. Can you meet me at Breadsmith's Café at 11:00? It's at the corner of Westwood and Detroit." I held my breath, hoping he'd agree. At the same time, my inner safety seeker hoped he'd decline.

"See you there."

That gave me more than enough time to get back to Breadsmith's and get us a table away from the counter, but close enough to other tables so customers would hear if I screamed for help. That meant, of course, assuming someone would come to my aid.

Telling Corrigan the plan flitted through my mind, but I decided against it. He'd either try to talk me out of it or insist on joining us. Either way, I wouldn't find out anything. Anyway, Gino had a rule: "Never let a cop bust into your action." I hoped in this case Gino was right.

My office phone rang just as I picked up my purse and was ready to go. It was Aunt Lena. The woman had to have a timetable noting the worst possible moments to call. But I had a few minutes and didn't want to regret not talking to her one last time before my possible demise.

"Hi Aunt Lena." My tone was as sing-song-y as a teen who'd been asked about their day at school.

I heard a loud harrumph and imagined her exhaling puffs of flour into the air.

"Claire Marie, you're a grown woman, but that doesn't give you permission to be out all hours of the night, worrying your family sick."

I looked to the ceiling. Put me before a firing squad and my aunt would insist I put on a sweater so as not to catch cold. "Sorry. I've been working, and let the time slip away. I'll be more mindful from now on. Promise. Is there anything you need?" I made a circular motion with my hand, like a television producer when he wants the actor to speed his monologue up.

"I'm having your father over for manicotti tomorrow night. You and Michael are invited."

I rubbed my face. "Nice try, Aunt Lena. But I'll be coming solo." Otherwise, we'd be singing West Side Story songs and cutting the manicotti with a circular saw.

She wasn't to be deterred. "But your father wants him to come."

Sure he does. "Sorry. Just not possible." I checked the time. "Hate to cut this short, but I've got an appointment I can't be late for. What time do you want me there?" We settled on my arriving at 6:00 and hung up.

I'd be cutting it close for my meeting with Michael at Breadsmith's but could still make it work. Then I heard footsteps stop at my door.

Chapter Twenty

I didn't move. *FedEx?* I swore the doorknob took ten seconds to turn. The door creaked open.

"Michael. What're you doing here?" I failed to keep my voice level, instead sounding like a wolf baying at the moon.

He closed the door behind him. "Your office number showed on my phone. Thought maybe we could talk here first. Alone."

Everything inside me froze. This was not going according to plan. I coughed to buy some time before responding. "But I'm just starving, and we can eat and talk at the same time."

Michael strode over to my desk and placed his hands flat down on it. "Let's talk now, please." He smiled, but it didn't soften his expression.

My hands squeezed the seat of my chair so tight, they'd have to be pried off. "Well, it's settled then. Talk first, eat second." Would he notice if I dug through my purse for my mace? Of course he would.

Without taking his eyes off me, he pulled up a chair

beside my desk. "What happened with Corrigan?"

"They've charged Eagleton with your sister's murder." Michael's face went blank and his hands dropped to his sides, limp. "You're relieved, aren't you?" I should've posed it in a different way, but he didn't seem to notice.

"Yes, but how did they…rather, why did he do it?"

My explanation didn't include any mention of the letters. That discussion was for when other people were around. I did explain the police's angle on Eagleton's motive.

Michael listened without a sound. When I finished, he sat back and stared at the wall behind me. "Then it's over."

"Yes, it is." I sat quietly for a moment, but he didn't add anything. My questions still lingered unanswered, but having ignored Corrigan's advice to get a gun, I refrained from asking them. The wrong answers could be dangerous, and I didn't want to hear them in a deserted office building. So, onto my ploy. "How about we go to Breadsmith's now? Something sweet would hit the spot."

He scratched his chin. "Could we do it tomorrow? I should notify someone about...you know…" His voice drifted off.

My mouth asked before my brain could stop it. "Who?"

His eyes darkened. Their mood didn't match his off-hand response. "Attorney."

He stood up to leave at the same time my phone rang.

It was Aunt Lena. What else could she possibly want? I held up one finger, as if to ask Michael to wait.

Her voice was sugar. "Hello dear. Just wanted to let you know I found Michael's phone number and left a message for him to come to dinner with you."

I wanted to lay my head down on my desk. "Why did you do that?"

She chuckled. "One day you'll thank me for this." *Yeah, as they fish my body out of Lake Erie.*

When the call ended, Michael said, "I heard. Please don't be embarrassed. I'd like to come if it's all right with you." He paused. "Now that Eagleton's been arrested, we can move on."

My fake smile probably made me look more queasy than happy. "Yeah, that'd be great." A romance with Michael seemed about as safe as holding hands with a grizzly. I chewed my lower lip. "How about I pick you up at 4:30 tomorrow and drive to my aunt's." Get to his place early and maybe talk him out of coming to dinner. The thought of him sitting there with my aunt and father made me want to claw out his eyes. What if instead of a bottle of wine, he brings a rope to give a new meaning to hanging around together? Whatever was necessary to stop that from happening, I'd do. Even digging for information without a crowd as a safety cushion.

After Michael left, my stomach felt jumpy like it knew something my brain didn't. Michael hadn't said anything about seeing his attorney before I told him about Eagleton. If he wasn't going there, where was he going?

I squinted at the far wall and it hit me. Ed. Now that Eagleton was in custody, would Ed still have a guard? I would've collapsed if I hadn't been sitting down. My fingers pushed the numbers of Corrigan's phone as fast as they could. Voice mail. If the devil himself chased me, I couldn't have made it out the door any speedier.

As in a miracle, every light was green. Ordinarily, I would spend five minutes or so trying to straighten my car in its parking space. This time, crooked would have to do. Rather than wait for the elevator, I dashed up the stairs to Ed's floor and, panting, speed-walked down the corridor. A uniformed guard sat outside Ed's room and my heart went back to its normal pace. I slouched against a wall, hands on knees to catch my breath.

My relief, though, was quickly shot through with worry. Where had Michael gone?

I swallowed my guilt for not stopping in to see Ed, but he'd understand. Back at my car, I tried to put the pieces together and formulate my strategy. First, something for my on-again-off-again headache. Leaning over to get some aspirin from my glove compartment, I spotted a man in the next parking lot row over. He flung his car door open like he wanted to rip it off, slid inside, gunned the engine, and sped away. It was Michael.

Adrenalin surged through me, preparing me for the chase. But what would I do if I caught him? Anyway, it was a moot point since that power surge my body felt didn't extend to my car. It was, as Gino would say, 'not in primo condition.' It huffed, coughed, and finally started, but by then Michael was long gone.

I pounded in Corrigan's number, thinking I needed to put him on speed dial. Damn. Voice mail again. The guy never answered his phone. "It's Claire. Michael just tore out of Fairview Hospital's parking lot. I can't follow him but maybe you can."

Then it hit me like a bucket of ice water. Was Ed still okay? What if Michael did something to him after I left? I ran back into the hospital, but this time took the elevator since one sat open, ready. A ride to the second floor never seemed so long. I pounded on the elevator button, whispering, "Come on. Come on."

Tears of relief filled my eyes at the sight of that same cop still sitting placidly in front of Ed's door. I couldn't stop myself from showing him my identification and entering Ed's room.

I stood at the head of Ed's bed, careful not to disturb the wires and tubes everywhere. "Wake up please, Ed." With a quick prayer for him to come out of the coma, I returned to my car.

To clear my mind, I leaned my head back against the headrest. Despite Corrigan's certainty Eagleton did it, to me everything pointed to Michael. He had the opportunity, but his motive remained unclear.

Corrigan had left a voice message for me. "I'm not about to chase after someone because you think they're up to no good. We've got the killer, remember? Anyway if your family issue is taken care of, please get back here and sign off on the assault charge. I'm waiting."

I didn't call him back.

My mind circled around and around, remembering my first meeting with Michael, then his confession about the letters, Mallorie's death, and Ed's attack. Even without knowing his motive, I'd bet my paltry bank account Michael was guilty.

Besides not knowing where he'd gone or what his motive was, another thing kept me uneasy. Dinner at my aunt's. Michael could not be a guest. Imagining Aunt Lena asking the murderer to say grace made my heart sick. No matter how the scenario played out, that dinner wasn't going to happen.

I called Aunt Lena to tell her Michael couldn't make it after all and since it was just the three of us, I'd take her and Dad to dinner at 4:00. This way no one would be there if Michael showed up on his own. How to pay for this dinner was still a mystery, though.

Aunt Lena picked up on the second ring. "Claire, honey. Got someone on the other line. I'll call you back." She hung up before I could say a word. As if it were the phone's fault, I squeezed and shook it in frustration, took a deep breath and tried my father. It went directly into voice mail. *Doesn't anyone answer their phones anymore?* Not wanting to spook him telephonically, I didn't leave a message. My only choice now was to call them both later.

I shifted in my car seat and made a decision, one I'd resisted. But the stakes were higher now. It was looking more like I'd have no choice in where my confrontation with Michael would happen. There might be nobody to come to my rescue, and my family was still at risk. Whatever could have set Michael off to kill Constance was still unknown, but now two people were dead and one was comatose. Despite my dread mixed with anxiety, I left to buy a gun.

In Ohio, I could buy a gun without a permit, so it was fairly easy to do. The harder part was learning how to shoot it. Gino did have a rule about guns: "Only pack heat if you plan to leave the other guy on ice."

The gun shop owner pointed me in the direction of a shooting range where someone showed me what to do. Annie Oakley I wasn't. My only hope was I'd never have to use the damn thing.

***

That evening I sat in my car and watched the solitary light that flickered upstairs in Michael's house. Maybe he was in his study, busy destroying evidence. My nerves had me fumbling as I loaded my gun. I meant to bring back the truth.

I wished Ed was with me. Or Corrigan. That reminded me to put in another call to the detective. He'd probably yell at me, but from the things he'd said, he'd rather lecture me on staying alive. My call went straight to his voicemail. I kept my voice even. "It's Claire, telling you I'm currently on a stake out at Michael's."

I'd been sitting in the dark for about five minutes when the upstairs light in the house went off. The front door opened and Michael stepped out, looked both ways, and went back in, closing the door behind him.

I ducked down fast and held my breath, hoping he hadn't seen me. He was up to something, that much was clear. I called Corrigan again, but it went to voicemail just like before. "Help!" I yelled into the phone.

It was surprisingly warm outside, but I felt chilled down into my soul. With a deep, ragged breath, I patted the gun in my pocket. Waiting was getting awfully tiresome. Knocking on Michael's door might shake things up. When he'd ask what I wanted, my gun would get him talking. *Yeah. Sure.* Or maybe Corrigan would arrive by then and stop Michael from wringing my neck for pulling a gun on him.

My thoughts continued along that path until Corrigan pulled up beside me and shone a flashlight in my eyes. "What the hell, DeNardo? Do I need to chain you to me to keep you out of trouble?"

Chained together someday may be fine, but not tonight. I hissed, "Michael is up to no good. Wait and see."

Corrigan turned off the flashlight. "You should have come back to the station to sign the assault charge against Eagleton. But no. You'd rather make a nuisance of yourself out here." He scowled. "I'm going to escort you home and stay there with you until you're sound asleep. That's the only way I can trust you to stay out of trouble."

"But, he's—"

"He's home, minding his own business, like you should be. Let's go."

I put my car in gear and purposely drove ten miles under the speed limit all the way home. Corrigan loved to speed, so this was my petty revenge. It took about fifteen minutes extra to get there, and I was still fuming.

He opened my apartment door and followed me in. "Okay, Claire, we can watch TV together or play cards, or whatever. Your choice."

"None of the above." I sniffed and pulled a diet soda for myself and grudgingly grabbed another one, thrusting it at him. He accepted with a smile.

I crashed down on the sofa, arms crossed. He joined me, grabbed the remote, and chose a comedy. His laugh was mellow, masculine. Had I been less peeved, the sound would've have been pleasing.

As if to tease me, he scooted closer. Cozy, but it didn't suit my mood. I snatched the remote and put the television on mute.

Wanting to have the height advantage, I stood. "How can you sit there, with Michael doing who-knows-what? He's already been at the hospital twice. He drugged me. *And* told me he wrote those threatening letters to his sister. He fooled me into thinking he didn't kill Constance so I didn't tell you about the letters." I put my hands out in case he wanted to cuff me. "Now you could arrest me for withholding evidence. But it's better than letting the real killer go loose."

Corrigan's face hardened. Had I gone too far with

accepting arrest? What if he thought throwing me in jail was a good idea? Did my cousin, Anthony, handle criminal cases anymore?

His phone rang and he took his time answering. "Yeah, be right there." After hanging up, he took my hands into his. "Got to go. Promise me you'll stay here until I come back."

A little alarm in my head told me this had to do with Constance's murder. "What if you're gone a long time, like until morning?" He took a deep breath, ready to say something, but I stopped him. "If what you're about to do has anything to do with Constance, Ed, or Michael, shouldn't you let me come along?" I watched his expression carefully to see if my suggestion had a chance.

It didn't. Without saying a word, he threw on his sport coat and straightened his tie. "It's police business." I frowned, and he softened. "But if this pans out, I'll come get you. So stay put."

The set of his jaw told me arguing would be of no use. "Promise." Besides, if I made him mad enough, he may not keep me informed.

"Lock the door behind me." He rushed out and I did as he said. This would be a long night.

Like so much else in this case, I was wrong. Less than five minutes after Corrigan left, something slammed against my door. A wave of nausea hit me as I recalled the sound of Mallorie's body slumped against my office door. This time though, the body could be Corrigan's.

I grabbed my new gun in my unsteady hands and yelled, “Who is it?” No surprise that no one answered. My eye up to the peephole provided no clues either.

I dialed 911 with my free hand, then held the phone up to my ear. Not knowing if someone was lying in the hallway, hurt, I unlocked the door but left the chain in place; no sense taking chances.

The hairs on my neck were on high alert and would’ve run off if they could. The door creaked as I cracked it open to peek out.

An arm I didn’t see slammed the door furiously against my hand, ripping the chain lock off the door. My gun and phone went flying toward the bathroom hallway. Before I could react, someone barreled into me, shoving me further into the room. Without taking his eyes off me, he locked my door behind him.

“Hello, Claire.”

My feet felt glued to the floor and my knees quivered so hard they knocked together. I swallowed hard. “Michael.”

Chapter Twenty-One

Michael motioned toward my sofa. “Please, sit down.” The twelve-inch blade of the knife in his hand glinted off the ceiling light.

My legs felt fifty pounds each as I backed up. They finally hit the cushion, and I collapsed, my eyes frantically scanning the area for my gun.

He lowered himself into the chair that sat catty-corner from the sofa. “Hate to break in on you like this. But you gave me no choice.”

I dug my fingers into the sofa cushion to steady myself. “Why are you here?”

Michael leaned forward. He clucked his tongue and slowly shook his head, like he felt sorry for me. “I really liked you, Claire. Thought you felt the same for me.”

To move away from the knife, I sank back. “I do, Michael.” My voice sounded calm, but my insides rocked and rolled.

He waved the knife at me like it was a pointer. “No. You spied on me.” He paused for a moment. “I trusted you. Even told you I wrote the letters to Constance." He almost pouted. "And you let me kiss you."

I rubbed the palm of my hand over my cheek where his lips had been, wishing I could remove the top layer of skin. Fearful of making things worse, I turned my grimace into a weak smile. "You were right to trust me, Michael. But as a private detective I've got to be ever vigilant and questioning."

He shook his head slowly, regret shadowing his face. "I tried to keep you safe. Pleaded with you to drop the case. Used my songs to warn you." He rubbed his forehead with his free hand. "Even drugged you to get you out of harm's way."

"But, how could I have known the trouble you went to?" I put my hands together as if praying. "Please, Michael…"

His eyes narrowed. "You don't believe Eagleton killed my sister. Do you?"

"Of course I do. You know, Corrigan is on his way here. Let's continue this conversation another time."

He shook his head and moved over to the sofa, sliding close enough to me his left thigh touched my right one. In an instant he twisted his torso, and grabbed me in a chokehold with one arm, holding the knife against my back with his other. "This is the last time."

His weapon could enter my back with the least bit of struggle. Best to keep him talking. "If you kill me, the cops will know Eagleton is innocent." My heart pounded so hard I felt the pressure in my temples.

"I've thought of that." His voice took on a Vincent Price quality. "But it'd be different if you committed suicide."

I whimpered. "You don't want to do this." *Clearly he did.*

"I *am* sorry." He pulled me to my feet.

"Wait!" *Stall.* "At least tell me why you hired me and then killed your sister." The knife shook in his hand, and I was terrified he'd cut me right then.

"I wanted her to know someone was watching her. So I hired you. I had to make sure she wouldn't go back on our deal. Her death was an accident. I didn't mean for her to die. If she just hadn't reneged."

Squirming and trying to loosen his grip on my arms didn't work. "Deal? For money? But you're already wealthy."

He sniffed. "*Was* wealthy. Bad investments."

"Biologic Solutions. Was the deal with them?"

"Smart girl. Yes." Sounding like a kid tattling, he added, "Eagleton and Sean Lawrence were part of it too." His voice grew sharp, resentful. "But Constance thought she was in love with Luther, and didn't want to betray him. So she betrayed me instead."

I wondered if *rigor mortis* would set in by the time Corrigan found me. "So what happened?"

"She'd already stolen the formula for a new youth-preserving drug. We were supposed to meet Bio Solutions and hand it over. We'd split the money." He tightened his lock on my neck and I gasped. "But

Constance hid the formula. She caught me tearing her office apart looking for it, and went after me. I pushed her out of the way and she fell." His voice broke and the knife broke my skin. I closed my eyes and bit my lip hard.

Michael's words were thick with emotion. "She hit her head on her desk corner. It was too late for me to do anything. She was already dead. I still needed the formula even more so I tore her office apart. It wasn't there."

He continued. "Mallorie saw everything. I couldn't afford to keep paying that bitch. She got what she deserved."

I wanted to rip this monster's head off, but contained my rage. "And Ed?" I whispered in a hoarse voice.

"An unavoidable casualty."

Fear made it hard to keep my mind from scattering. "Does it get easier each time?"

He spoke as if involved in a philosophical conversation, "You could say it does grow on you."

"But you can't keep killing people."

He pulled me up. "You're right. You'll be the last. Assuming your friend, Ed, doesn't wake up." He maneuvered us toward the bathroom.

I teetered and almost lost my balance, but he held me up, increasing the pressure on my throat. I was lightheaded, but needed to keep it together. "The break-in at your home? Was that to throw suspicion off you?"

He exhaled loudly, annoyed. "Yes." He yanked me

back. "No more questions."

"Please, Michael, don't do this."

"No choice."

Now or never. I pushed back into him as hard as I could. Occupied with maintaining his balance his knife drooped slightly. I stepped onto his foot and mashed my heel in.

He yelped in pain and the knife clattered to the floor. Able to break free, I dove for my gun, spun around and aimed it. This would've been a great time for Corrigan to get back. Didn't happen.

Michael stared at the weapon and his face went from red to white. "You can't shoot me." He took a slight step toward me and I took one backwards.

The gun seemed to gain weight as I held it. When one hand waivered. I clutched it with both. "I will if I have to. Don't make me, please." *Could I really?* I didn't want to find out. "We're going back to the living room and calling the police."

He didn't move.

I readjusted the gun in my hands. "Let's go."

He placed one foot toward the living room. Instead of continuing in that direction, he lunged at me. His hand dug into mine as we struggled for the gun. A shot fired into the toilet tank. It exploded and water gushed everywhere.

We tussled for a moment. Then with a final yank, he wrestled the gun from me. As I let go, he stumbled back, lost his balance and conked his head on the counter. I snatched the gun from his limp hand and held it on him.

Breathless, I said, "Get up."

No response. I nudged him with the toe of my shoe. No reaction.

Then I did the dumbest thing in the history of private investigatordom: I bent down to see if he was conscious.

His hand shot up and he grabbed for the gun, but I gave the weapon a tug using all my remaining strength. To keep possession, he wrapped his hand around the barrel. My finger was on the trigger and the gun went off once more. This time the bullet threw him back as it slammed into his chest.

Chapter Twenty-Two

Blood everywhere. I yanked a towel off the bar and pushed it against his leaking wound then began rising to recover the 911 call. But he squeezed my wrist.

His voice was weak and thin. "Best to die here." With that, his eyelids drooped and his hand dropped away. He released a final shudder and was gone.

I collapsed back onto my rear and clasped my knees to my chest. Tears streamed down my face. At almost the same time, I laughed out loud because I was alive. But the laughter quickly morphed into a hoarse sob. I covered his face with the towel and stepped away to call 911. But didn't need to. A siren screamed nearby, followed quickly by a pounding on my door.

A familiar, welcome voice. "Police. Open up."

I sprang to the door and flung it open. Corrigan's eyes grew wide when he saw blood splattered all over me. His hands flew to my shoulders.

"It's Michael's."

Corrigan's shoulders dropped with relief. "We got

your 911 call. Where is he?"

"In there." I pointed my thumb toward the bathroom. "We struggled. He's dead." I lowered my head, not wanting Corrigan to see the tears that had started anew. Bad enough he'd noticed my shivering. He guided me to the sofa, took off his suit jacket, and wrapped it around my shoulders.

A couple of uniformed cops walked in and headed to the bathroom. Corrigan followed. "I'll be right back, Claire."

A short time later, Corrigan bent down next to me, his voice hushed and gentle. "Can I get you something? Water, diet pop? How about a washcloth?"

I shook my head to the soda, but gratefully accepted the wet cloth. Corrigan pulled out his small notepad and a pen. "Are you able to give your statement now?" He placed his hand over mine. "Take your time."

Halfway through retelling what happened, my mouth dried out and I asked for a diet soda, but would have rather have had a shot of whiskey. Finally finished, I was proud to have gotten through my statement with only one breakdown.

The coroner arrived, did his exam, and Michael's body was taken away. The gun and knife were placed in evidence bags.

"Will I be arrested?"

"No, but you may be asked more questions. You'll be fine, though." Corrigan helped me up. I swayed, but he held me firmly. He smiled and the warmth reached his eyes. "Someone would like to see you." He looked at my torn and bloody clothes and frowned. "Maybe you'd like to clean up first."

I scrubbed my face and hands, then all the way up to my elbows until they felt raw. I went into the adjoining bedroom and threw on some jeans and a top. Zipping up my jeans, Michael's shooting came back to me and I burst into tears. Cries so strong it felt like they'd rip my gut apart. I fell back onto my bed, curled up and rocked back and forth.

Corrigan rapped on my door. "Are you all right?"

A wobbly, "Give me a minute," came out. I swallowed the last of the sobs, and wiped the dampness from my cheeks with the back of my hand, and splashed water on my face to hide the tear tracks. The final touch was some lipstick.

Corrigan had parked himself so close to my bedroom door I almost ran into him. He took in my puffy face but made no comment. We didn't talk until we got into his car.

His hands firmly on the steering wheel, Corrigan looked straight ahead. "Some say the first is the toughest. I say anytime you have to shoot someone it's hard."

"Is that supposed to make me feel better?"

"Does it?"

"No."

He shrugged. "Then I guess it wasn't. It was just to let you know this stuff isn't easy."

There was no fitting response to that and we

continued down the road in silence. Every so often, Corrigan would look like he wanted to spout wise advice, but each time, stopped himself. That was fine with me. I had a hole inside that no words could fill.

Eventually it dawned on me where we were headed. "Did something happen with Ed?" *Please, please let him be alive.*

The corners of the detective's mouth turned up. "He's awake and talking."

My hands came together and my throat produced joyous sounds. Not words exactly, more like happy sighs. At last, something good. Fidgeting like a kid in a brand new Sunday suit, I barely waited until Corrigan turned off the car's engine before popping open my car door. Inside the hospital, I took two steps at a time until arriving on the second floor and Ed's room.

His eyes were closed. Hoping he hadn't lost consciousness again, I tiptoed up to him and whispered, "Ed?"

His face broke into a wide grin and he opened his eyes. "Hey." He sounded like he'd scratched his throat with tree bark.

I leaned over and brushed his stubbly cheek with my lips. "So good to see you, you know…"

"Back among the living?" He snorted but it turned into a rough cough. He took a sip of water. "Corrigan arrest Adler yet? He killed his sister over a phony formula that never would've worked."

A heavy weight descended on me again and I bit my

lower lip. "Michael's dead."

Ed shifted in his bed. "No kidding? How?"

Corrigan chose that minute to come into Ed's room. "Claire figured him for the killer."

In a solemn voice, I recounted what happened.

Ed licked his lips. "That's tough, but better him than you, kiddo."

A nurse bustled into Ed room. "Mr. Horwath needs to rest. You'll have to come back another day."

I squeezed Ed's hand. "I'll be back tomorrow."

Corrigan chimed in, "That'll make two of us."

Ed nodded. "Before you go, after my rehab or whatever they're gonna do with me, I want to take on another job. Ya know, you and me, Claire. We make a helluva team."

I stood motionless. Both of us had barely gotten away with our lives. True, we did survive. But what if that was just beginner's luck? Did I want to tempt fate? Could I deal with more death, not to mention being scared more often than not?

Both guys waited for my response. Not wanting to say the wrong thing, I hesitated, twisting my mouth from side to side. Then shrugged. *So I'd be scared. Balloons scare me too and I still go to birthday parties. Of course a balloon probably couldn't kill me. But now I had a gun and sort of knew how to use it. Besides, my desire to see justice done would certainly be met. Why not give it a try?*

"If you're sure you want to do it, that'd be great, Ed.

We'll have to discuss money later."

He smirked. "Yeah, maybe we do it on the layaway plan."

Corrigan scowled. "If you two are staying in business together, I better keep an eye on you."

But he was clearly looking at me.

Recipes…

Aunt Lena's Meatballs and *Sugo* (Sauce)

Sugo

1 clove of garlic, minced
1 12 oz can tomato paste
3 C of water
½ tsp salt
¼ tsp pepper
1 tsp dried basil or 2 tsp fresh basil
1 tsp dried oregano or 2 tsp fresh oregano
Pinch of granulated sugar (optional)

Add enough olive oil to cover the bottom of your pan. Add all other ingredients and simmer for 1-2 hours. Stir occasionally.

Meatballs

1 lb lean ground beef
½ tsp salt
1-2 tsp fresh parsley or a pinch if using dried parsley
1 egg
3 Tbsp Romano cheese
¼ C breadcrumbs (add cold water to make this into ½ C breadcrumbs)

Add all ingredients together and mix. To shape mixture into balls, keep hands wet. Pan fry meatballs at medium heat until browned on all sides, about 5 minutes if they're the size of golf balls. Add meatballs to sugo to heat through.

Dear Reader,

If you enjoyed this book, please recommend it to a friend. Even lend your copy to them!

Reviews are always welcome. They help other readers discover your favorite books. If you do write one for The Terrified Detective: Plateful of Murder, please let Carole know. She'd like to thank you personally. Her email is: cmsldfowkes@gmail.com

Sign up for Carole's Newsletter to get insider information, sneak peeks, contests and freebies, and to be the first to hear when her next book is coming out. Since these newsletters only come out a few times a year, you won't be inundated with them. Also, rest assured, Carole doesn't sell email addresses.

The link for her Newsletter is: http://eepurl.com/8xC5L

For more information on Carole, visit her website. www.carolefowkes.com

If you enjoyed this first book in the Terrified Detective cozy mystery series, make sure you check out Book Two which is available now.

Killer Cannoli

Chapter One

"Sorry, Claire, but he doesn't look like a 'Larry' to me." My father folded the dish towel and set it on the blue and yellow Formica countertop he and my late mother had installed. His bushy black-and-grey eyebrows knitted together.

I shrugged. "Maybe it's a nickname." I slouched on one of my dad's checkered kitchen chairs in his circa 1970's kitchen and loosened my belt. I regretted the extra helping of hot, crusty bread I'd had. Not for the first time I wished I'd inherited my dad's eat-it-all, never-gain-weight metabolism instead of my mother's walk-by-food, gain-five-pounds one. At 5'2" sixteen ounces made the difference between comfortably wearing my jeans and having those red wrinkle lines on my hips from the material digging in. Now that I was 31, it was harder to keep at 107 pounds.

I pulled my thoughts back to my dad's concerns. "Anyway, is that why you don't like him?"

"Part of it. He's hiding something and that makes him no good for your Aunt Lena." He pointed his index finger to make his point. "Someone should warn her." Staring right into my eyes he said, "Claire, honey…"

I leaned back and threw up my hands. "Oh no. Not me." Aunt Lena, my late mother's sister, ran one of the best Cleveland area Italian eat-in bakeries, *Cannoli's*, and a better person you'll never meet. She had a temper, though and when she got mad, junkyard dogs are less intimidating than she is. But then, what if my dad was right and this guy, Larry, was up to no good? As a private investigator, was I responsible for my relatives' poor choices in dating? I didn't want to be, but Dad's insistence that Larry was bad news told me I was. Just thinking about my Aunt Lena's wrath at my interference made me cringe.

I put my arms around my dad's neck. "I'll run a background check. If it looks like your hunch is good, I'll do some investigating. If he's an undesirable, then I'll break it to Aunt Lena, over the phone, where she can't get to me."

"Isn't there more you could do?" My father's face lit up. "Maybe you could get that detective to help."

I acted like I didn't know who he meant. "Which detective?"

My dad looked at me like I'd claimed to be Swedish. "You know. The one who took us to lunch. He helped you on that other case."

I wrinkled my nose. "Oh. Him." Of course Dad meant Brian Corrigan. That good-looking, blonde, blue-eyed unmentionable man who had flirted with me. That same detective who, after the Adler murder case, said he'd call and never did. Now I'd rather eat mushy pasta than ask him for help. "I'm sure he's busy, Dad. I don't want to bother him." *Choke him, yeah. Bother him, no.*

I don't know if my dad figured it out, but he didn't pursue the subject. "Okay. Check his background. But you have to see him too." His face hardened, like when Johnny Zysinsky threw a rock and broke our front window. "Don't be like your aunt and get taken in by Larry, or whatever his real name is."

"Don't worry. I can get a look at him and still keep my distance." I planned to check out Larry from behind the counter at *Cannoli's*. Safer that way.

I left my father's house shortly afterwards, carrying a covered dish of manicotti he'd made especially for me. The smells of melted mozzarella and ricotta cheese mixing with tomatoes, basil and oregano filled my car. Ordinarily, that'd soothe me, like soft music calms dental patients. Not this time. Being the uncourageous person I am, paying attention to my gut feelings is the best way to keep myself out of conflict and danger. This time it screamed to avoid Larry. But I couldn't do that. My duty to watch out for my family drowned out the noise.

Hoping I'd be too busy to go to *Cannoli's* for a talk with my Aunt Lena just yet, I checked my voicemails. Not one message. I stuck out my lower lip and blew a breath into my bangs. Still wanting to delay this unpleasant business, I decided to stop at my office anyway and put the pasta in my small fridge. Maybe when I arrived, there'd be some frantic soon-to-be client waiting there to see me, pacing and checking the time over and over. Or one waving a fat check around, of course, begging me to find his lover who'd disappeared the previous week. I snorted.

I started my car and imagined a scenario in which Larry was actually some big-time gambler wanted by the Mob and beautiful women everywhere. The idea entertained me, thinking about my aunt with someone like that. It also prevented me from worrying about the reason for my visit to Aunt Lena's bakery.

She was in *Cannoli's* kitchen when I got there. Instead of being covered in flour and banishing her coarse black hair back into her hairnet, she was putting on lipstick. The color could best be described as 'sure-I'm-older-but-still-sexy' red. More surprising, she had on a new dress with tiny beads. It was black and had probably been advertised as 'suitable for dates or funerals.'

Before I could manage a greeting, she grabbed my wrist and whispered, "Larry's here." Her face showed all the excitement of a game show winner. She dabbed at her lips. "How do I look?"

I took in her abundant cleavage, overgenerous waistline, and dimpled arms and kissed her cheek. "The man doesn't stand a chance."

She blushed and giggled like a girl might the first time she's kissed. My heart melted as I realized this warrior of a woman who held down a business and kept us all, including my widowed father, in line could have a tender side.

I turned away so she wouldn't see my face cloud with worry. If this guy hurt her, I'd make sure he incurred some injury himself. I chuckled when I realized that if he did do Aunt Lena wrong, he'd probably end up with a dent in his head from her rolling pin.

She hesitated at the door leading to the pastry counter and tables and pulled herself up straight, breasts out, stomach in as much as possible. She whispered. "Wish me luck."

I crossed my fingers for luck. "Knock him dead." Hoping I could catch some of their conversation, I threw on an apron and followed her to the pastry area.

Aunt Lena's friend and part-time employee, Angie, was already there. She nodded her hello to me and out of the side of her mouth added, "You here to see your aunt in action?"

"Yes. No...." I didn't want to tell her I was spying for my dad's benefit. "I want to talk to this guy. My aunt hadn't been on the dating scene since she met my Uncle Tommy in the 1960's and he passed away over ten years ago."

"If you want my opinion, Lena could do better." Angie tilted her head toward the back table. My aunt had just joined a man who was already seated.

I had to stop myself from wincing. Larry was not an attractive man. In fact with his pale coloring, long, pointed nose and tiny eyes, he looked like a white laboratory rat. I wondered how fast he could run through a maze. My nose curled up as I watched him nibble on a croissant. It was more than his looks that set my neck hairs at attention though. It was the incongruity. His pants shouted 'cheap polyester' and his shirt, a flowered leftover from the disco era, was unbuttoned to where it shouldn't have been. His shoes looked one step away from the trash bin. But he wore two pinkie rings with diamonds bigger than the ones in my late mother's wedding ring.

"Angie, you've met him. What do you think?" I whispered.

"His hair and skin are so pale he looks like he died about the same time as Lena's Tommy. And those clothes. Let's just say he doesn't follow fashion trends."

I stifled a laugh as two customers approached the counter and I stepped up to wait on them but my phone vibrated.

Angie waved me away. “Go on, it might be one of your clients. I’ll handle this.”

I gave her a grateful smile and hoped she was right. But it wasn’t a client.

“Hey, kiddo. Ed.”

Ed Horwath was my new part-time assistant. Not that my business needed one since I’d only had one big case so far. That’s when I met Ed and he, in turn, almost got killed because of me. Another story, though. He’s a security guard, but works for me when I need some muscle. Or an extra body.

“What’s up?” I hoped he wasn’t looking for an assignment. To tell the truth, I was still a little uneasy around Ed. He grew up in a tough part of Cleveland and while he swore he never punched anyone unless it was necessary, I think his definition of the term ‘necessary’ was different than mine was.

Lately my business had shrunk from being bad to pitiful. What was even more pathetic was the type of cases. Take for example Gloria Wellsing, my latest client. She had me investigating who was secretly feeding her purebred Husky, Sheba, table scraps and making her fat. I couldn’t even admit to Ed I’d taken that job, but a girl’s got to eat. Maybe if I found who fed Sheba, I could wrestle some of the scraps away.

Ed cleared his throat. “Been pretty dull around here. Need some excitement. Got any for me?”

“Sorry, Ed. Nothing’s come in.”

"Okay. See ya." He sounded like a kid who finds out the roller coaster has been closed for repairs. But I couldn't do anything about it.

I turned back just in time to see Aunt Lena shake rat-man's hands and head toward the kitchen. Angie nudged me hard. "Find out what happened."

I waited a moment so as not to appear too nosey, then strolled back into the kitchen. Aunt Lena's face was flushed and she wiped a bead of sweat from her forehead. "Damn menopause." She picked up a towel and fanned herself with it.

I grabbed her by the elbows. "So how'd it go?"

She leaned back, pretending to be blasé about it all. "He asked me out for tonight. I said yes."

I coughed, so the words, "Oh my Lord, what were you thinking?" wouldn't escape my lips.

She raised an eyebrow. "Hmm. Maybe you don't think he's Mr. Charming, but I do. I have more mature tastes." She grabbed her apron and put it on. "Besides, he's not a no-account who has nothing. And he's practical. Says he's got real good insurance. Now, tell me to have a good time."

I grabbed her by the elbows. "Promise me you'll play hard to get."

She put her hands on her hips. "A smart woman knows what a man wants. Never mind what he thinks he wants."

I had no desire to know which was which so I changed directions. "Where's he taking you?"

He'll meet me here at 7:00, after we close then dinner somewhere."

My phone again. This time it was Dad, probably to ask me about Larry. I let it go to voicemail. "Aunt Lena, that's exciting." *Maybe you should bring a piece of cheese.* "My phone's going crazy. I better get back to the office." I kissed her damp cheek. "Have fun tonight."

I turned the key in my car's ignition. Nothing but an irritating whirr. I tried it twice more. No difference. I couldn't blame old Bob. He had over 190,000 miles and probably dreamed of retirement. But I couldn't afford to replace him. Every day I hopped into his rust-covered body and prayed his tired engine would turn over, but I feared this time he'd run his last. Thank God I was wrong and with a congested huff, he started up. We sputtered along and I tried to figure a way to afford a newer car. I quivered inside every time I thought about Bob heaving a last gasp on a dark, deserted road.

My phone rang. My dad again.

I barely said hello when he started. "So what do you think of *Larry*?" Sarcasm dripped with this last word.

"Didn't talk to him. I didn't want to cut in on Aunt Lena's action. He looked normal if you like rodents with poor taste in clothes, but I'll do that background check on him when I get back to the office." I hesitated for a moment then dropped the bomb. "She has a date with him tonight."

"She's out of her mind. We need to do a *che cosa*? An intervention."

"Don't do anything until you hear from me. Promise?"

He huffed. "Sorry, Pumpkin. It's just…she's your mother's sister and Theresa, God bless her, would strike me from heaven if I let something happen to Lena."

My heart went out to my dad. Mom had been gone less than four years. He was still learning to live without her and at the same time, deal with Aunt Lena. Aunt Lena, who thought it was her mission to smother my dad in her unique bossy way, with food and advice. Now he wanted to protect her. I pulled into my office parking lot. "Call you as soon as I find something. Okay?"

I opened the door to my office, flicked on my computer and started to dig into the life of Larry Walters. Except there wasn't any information to be had.

Killer Cannoli

Private Investigator Claire DeNardo visits her Aunt Lena's café, Cannoli's, and discovers a romance brewing between her aunt and a new customer. Claire's suspicions that he's lying about his identity prove solid when he's found dead at the café. Claire ignores the warnings of Police Detective Brian Corrigan and delves into the dead man's life. In the process, she realizes her aunt may unwittingly possess what the killer wants. And it's not her tiramisu recipe.

Bake Me a Murder

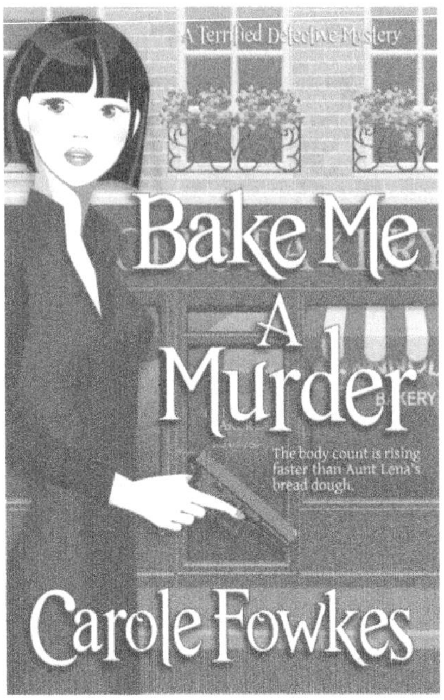

Private Investigator Claire DeNardo reluctantly takes on a case presented by her part-time employee, Ed. Ed's cousin, Merle, is searching for his former girlfriend, a topless dancer who ran with a rough crowd. But it's too late. The woman has been killed and Merle, who is now Claire's client, is arrested. When Claire digs into the victim's past, she uncovers a thriving illegal drug trade. Her fears about this case double when she learns about the mobster who is behind the unlawful business. All this while dodging Police Detective Brian Corrigan's determined efforts to get her off the case and into his arms.

Acknowledgements

I want to thank my husband, Greg, for his support, ideas, and patience. Nikki Salupo and Joanne Moore both stepped up when I needed their help most. Patience Jackson, Rae-Dawn Brightman, and Bill Payne lent their expertise to my efforts. Huge thanks goes to Kathleen Baldwin, whose advice, assistance, and reassurances made the publishing of this book possible.

Made in the USA
Monee, IL
07 December 2022

20067871R00144